Dreams
of a
Dancing
Horse

Catch all the

Angus MacMouse Brings Down the House
Linda Phillips Teitel

The Pup Who Cried Wolf
Chris Kurtz

Monkey See, Monkey Zoo
Erin Soderberg

Dreams of a Dancing Horse
Dandi Daley Mackall

Dreams
of a
Dancing
Horse

Dandi Daley Mackall

illustrations by Guy Francis

BLOOMSBURY

NEW YORK BERLIN LONDON SYDNEY

First published in the United States of America in October 2011
by Bloomsbury Books for Young Readers
www.bloomsburykids.com

For information about permission to reproduce selections from this book, write to
Permissions, Bloomsbury BFYR, 175 Fifth Avenue, New York, New York 10010

Library of Congress Cataloging-in-Publication Data
Mackall, Dandi Daley.
Dreams of a dancing horse / by Dandi Daley Mackall. — 1st U.S. ed.
        p.   cm.
Summary: Fred, a plow horse on an Oklahoma farm, dreams of being Federico
the Dancing Horse, but his antics cause trouble and he is sent away, to seek not only his
dream but a home where he might truly belong.
ISBN 978-1-59990-626-3 (paperback) • ISBN 978-1-59990-627-0 (hardcover)
[1. Dance—Fiction.   2. Horses—Fiction.   3. Home—Fiction.
4. Voyages and travels—Fiction.]   I. Title.
PZ7.M1905Dre 2011   [Fic]—dc22   2011005205

Book design by Yelena Safronova
Typeset by Westchester Book Composition
Printed in the U.S.A. by Quad/Graphics, Fairfield, Pennsylvania
2 4 6 8 10 9 7 5 3 1 (paperback)
2 4 6 8 10 9 7 5 3 1 (hardcover)

All papers used by Bloomsbury Publishing, Inc., are natural, recyclable products
made from wood grown in well-managed forests. The manufacturing processes
conform to the environmental regulations of the country of origin.

For Cassandra Eve Hendren—
dance, Cassie, dance!

Contents

Born to Dance

You might not believe me, but I was born to dance. Yes, yes, I know. I am the biggest horse you've ever seen. Head as large as a sack of grain. Hooves the size of dinner plates.

But never you mind. I, Federico, was created to feel the music of the spheres deep down in my horsey soul.

From the minute I could stand on all four of my wobbly colt legs, I could hear music. It reached into every part of me, from my scraggly forelock to my shaggy fetlocks.

"Hey! Fred! Watch where you're going up there, you big lug!"

That rude fellow is Round Rollo Quagmire, the driver of this plow and the son of Herbert Quagmire, owner of Quagmire Farms. Rollo looks like a haystack with legs. Coarse yellow hair, beady eyes, and a round body.

"Giddyup, Fred!" Rollo screams, snapping his whip.

Quagmire Farms is a small operation with a one-horse plow. Young Rollo is shouting at me. Humans have always insisted on calling me Fred.

I force myself to put one giant hoof in front of the other. But inside, I am imagining each step as part of a grand dance.

There! Hear the cry of that mourning dove? As always, I can't stop my neck from swaying and my mane from waving, even in this still and windless Oklahoma heat.

In the next pasture, cows are mooing. The music of it sets my hooves to shuffling in a four-four time: *shush, shush, shush, shush.*

Dogs bark in the distance, and my legs pick up the cha-cha beat: *bark, bark, bark-bark-bark; bark, bark, bark-bark-bark.*

"What a clumsy nag!" Rollo yells, snapping his reins on my rump.

Humans.

It's always been the same story. Why, I've been sold as Fred the Plow Horse and passed from farm to farm since the day I was born.

Humans aren't the only problem either. I've never fit in with the other plow horses I've worked with. Not that I haven't tried, mind you.

At Willow Creek Farms, the plow horses accused me of putting on airs. But seriously, was it my fault if I was never at home plowing? Federico was destined to dance, not to plow.

At the Equestrian Center outside Oklahoma City, where I got assigned field-plowing duties, there were gorgeous Lipizzans and Thoroughbreds in the main stable. Plow horses were housed in the old barn. I didn't complain. And still, most—though not all—of those plow horses teased me for walking and talking like the upper-class horses in the main stable.

I tried to get along with my coworkers. Honestly, I did. "Please don't get me wrong," I begged my barn mates after enduring a week of heckling from them. "You're all wonderfully fine fellows, and I'm ever so proud to work alongside you."

"Oh, listen to the gentleman, will you?" said Pogo, the lead plow horse. "Fred is ever so proud of us fine fellows."

"Doesn't that make you feel warm and fuzzy all over?" joked Pogo's harness partner, Big Pal.

The horse laughs that followed rocked the old barn.

How I yearned to fit in with my fellow workers! But I simply did not. Inside, I felt more kinship with the fine-boned dancing horses. They moved on the outside exactly the way I felt on the inside. They pranced, their hooves light as air, bounding on the dirt as if on springs. That's how I, Federico, move whenever I hear music.

When I heard a piano playing from the big house, notes galloping after one another in a mad chase, I could have galloped as fast as the Thoroughbreds. What did it matter that the race horses were sleek and lean, or that I towered over them, bigger than any of the plow horses on the grounds? The music raced through my veins, and I chased after it.

The beautiful Lipizzan performing horses shone white as the fluffiest clouds in the sky. I am painfully aware that my own coat is the dull brown of mud and common dirt. Yet when I heard violins and flutes coming from one of the house windows, my thick haunches became powerful but light. My forelegs transformed into instruments of dance, as graceful as the Lipizzan dancing horses.

But on the dry, red dirt of an Oklahoma field, it was a different story. Fred the Plow Horse was the last horse any creature wanted to be paired with in front of a plow. My knobby legs were hairy tree trunks that stumbled over each other as I walked the rows of dirt, jerking the plow behind me.

And so, after having been bounced from partner to partner at a series of farms and behind an endless number of plows, I have ended up here at Quagmire Farms. It is only my first day at the plow, and already I know that Herbert Quagmire, Rollo's father, is my hardest owner yet.

"Get moving, you old plug!" Round Rollo shouts. "Pick up your feet, and stop swaying!"

He flicks his leather whip, snapping it against my rump. "What kind of a plow horse are you anyway? You're the clumsiest creature I've ever seen."

For a second, I can't help wincing. His words sting more than the whip. Could this young fellow be right? After all, even plow horses think I'm Fred, the clumsiest plow horse they ever worked with. What if . . . ?

No! I blink away the sweat that's trickled into my eyes. Of course I'm clumsy in the field, harnessed to a plow. Why wouldn't I be? My moves weren't designed for plowing. I wasn't meant to plow fields into neat rows. I was meant to dance.

Turn me loose and set my world to music. Then they'd see. All my clumsiness would disappear.

I shut out the sound of Rollo's voice and call up the song that is always in my heart. My mother's song.

Just before my mother died, when I was no more than a foal, she told me, "You will always have my song in your heart, so I will never be far from you. Follow your heart and dance, my Federico."

Now, under the glaring midday sun, I throw

my shoulders into my work and do my best to pull the plow behind me to the beat of my mother's song.

I am not Fred the Plow Horse. I am Federico the Dancing Horse.

Crystalina the Ballerina

I always have trouble sleeping my first night in a strange barn, and tonight is no exception. The Quagmire barn smells like chickens and moldy grain. As far as I can tell, I'm the only horse in here.

I have always attempted to count my blessings instead of my complaints. So now I try not to think about how hungry I am, how small my new stall is, or how lonely it is in here with no other plow horse in sight.

Instead, in my head I make music out of the sound of crickets chirping, the buzz of a pesky horsefly, the swish of my tail swatting said horsefly, and . . .

Humming?

I'm almost certain that I hear humming. *Human* humming.

"Hum dee dum de dum hmmm hummm."

The soft notes make my heart spin. It's all I can do not to burst into dance right here, right now.

Then I see her. The notes are coming from a little human. A girl barely bigger than a newborn filly is humming in the dark. And she's not just humming. She's dancing.

The barn is dark, except for a streak of moonlight that floods the path in front of the stalls. The girl twirls and spins, as if she's floating on the moonbeam.

I hold my breath as the girl spins my way. Her arms sway gracefully above her head, and she twists her way up the aisle, barefoot and dancing on her toes. It's the most beautiful sight I've ever seen. How could I have imagined such a thing would appear in this shabbiest of barns?

For a second, I wonder if she could be an angel . . . although I would have thought angels

dressed better. She's wearing jeans that have holes in them and might better fit Round Rollo. They're so big that the poor, thin waif has tied a string of hay twine around her waist to hold up her pants.

Closer and closer she comes. And the closer she gets, the more light shines from her green eyes. With tiny flutter kicks, she dances from side to side until she's directly in front of me.

The girl stops. She looks startled, as if she'd been thinking there was no one in the world except her and her music. I recognize that look. I know that feeling.

"Well, hey there, big fella!" She smiles at me and comes as close as she can on the other side of my stall gate. "You must be the new horse I heard Uncle Herbert and Cousin Rollo going on about."

I'm grateful that she said "horse" and not "plow horse." Humans almost always assume a horse as big as I am must be a plow horse.

I wish I could tell her what a wonderful dancer she is and how much I enjoyed her song. But I have learned over the years that humans can only understand humans. And not even all humans. It is one of life's great mysteries.

The girl reaches over the stall door and strokes my forehead. "I already know your name. Rollo called you Fred when he reported to his daddy about your first day in the field. I won't tell you what he said or what other names he called you, but I didn't believe a word of it. That boy lies like a rug. If his lips are moving, he's a-lying. Truth is, Cousin Rollo is about as useless as a sore thumb. He and his daddy—my uncle Herbert—are both meaner than a pack of wet panthers.

"Anyway, Fred, my name is Lena, and I'm mighty pleased to know you."

I nicker and hope Lena knows that a nicker is a horse's most friendly greeting.

She shakes her head. "I'm just plumb sorry about Cousin Rollo. I reckon he's no bargain behind your plow, him not having the good sense God gave a goose and all. Even his daddy admits that boy is about as useful as a steering wheel on a mule."

I like the way she talks. The twang and her quaint expressions, even though I can't say I entirely understand what she's saying.

Lena stands on her tiptoes, and I wonder if she's about to twirl away from me. Instead, she reaches up and scratches me behind the ears. It's the very place I most love to be scratched.

"Can I tell you a secret?" Lena asks.

I nod.

She grins, wide eyed. "Did you just nod?"

I do it again.

"Are you really saying yes? I mean, did you understand me about telling you a secret?"

This time I nod four times. Sometimes it takes humans a bit of effort to understand.

"Well, if that's not the bee's knees! You can hog-tie me and call me Mabel!" she declares.

I admit to a bit of confusion of my own. I was certain she said her name was Lena.

"Well, that's right fine. That's what that is." She squints into my eyes like she can see through my head to my tail.

"So about that secret. My *real* name is Crystalina." She gets a faraway look in her sparkling eyes. "Sometimes I pretend I'm Crystalina the Ballerina."

That's what her turns and twists were. Ballet. This girl *should* be a ballerina. If she could understand horse, I'd tell her so right now.

The light goes out from her eyes like a candle's flame blown to smoke. "But it could never happen. I'm an orphan. Poor as a church mouse. Folks think Uncle Herbert was some kind of saint for taking me in when my ma and pa died. I reckon they'd just have to spend one day watching what goes on around here to know Uncle Herbert is no saint, no how. I do all the cleaning and cooking and most of the chores. That's why they keep me on.

"It pains me to say it, Fred, him being kinfolk and all. But that man is a no-account, as ornery as a hound dog and tighter than a fiddle string. Besides which, he doesn't have a bit of horse sense!"

She laughs at that one, and so do I. Even her laughter is musical, the rise of her high notes sweeping up from her bass. I have a hearty horse laugh myself, which seems to amuse her even further, making her tiny body shake with more laughter. That makes me laugh, which sets her off in a fresh bout of laughter, which makes me laugh again . . . And so it goes. I don't know when I've laughed like this. Maybe never.

When our laughter finally fades, Lena continues. "I think I've always had a hankering to dance, Fred. I used to dream about being a ballerina. I don't dream anymore. But I still like to dance. And this barn at night is the only place I can do it without getting into more hot water than a kettle. So I hope you don't mind me dropping in on you from time to time."

She stays in the barn for a while, scratching and petting me. And humming.

When neither of us can keep our eyes open, she yawns and says, "Nighty night, Fred. Sleep tight. Don't let the bedbugs bite."

I watch her drag herself back up the aisle. And still, she does a pirouette before waving a final good-bye.

Once Lena is gone, I check for the bedbugs she warned me about, but I don't find a one. Still, I sleep standing up.

And I think about Lena. She is without a doubt the nicest human I have ever encountered.

By the time morning comes and the sun peeks over the flat horizon beyond the barn, I have come to a conclusion: I must find a way to help Lena dream again. I have to help her become Crysta-lina the Ballerina.

Work Horse

This morning when Rollo comes to harness me to the plow, I make an extra effort to get a thorough look at him. I admit that I had stopped paying much attention to my drivers since most humans look remarkably alike.

But this fellow is an exception. He is round, with greasy hair that looks a great deal like his straw hat. Half-closed, beady snake eyes sink into his pudgy face. The snake appearance is further carried out by his boots, which appear to have come from the skins of a family of rattlesnakes.

It hardly seems possible that this fellow is part

of the same species as Lena, much less part of the same family.

"Get a move on, you lazy lug!" Round Rollo shouts. "Hey! Hold still, you ugly nag!" he whines in his next breath.

Talk about mixed messages.

He struggles with my harness, pulling some straps too tight and leaving others to flop.

Once we're out in the field, things go from bad to worse. It's impossible to know which way he intends to plow. He pays no attention to the dry field. Instead, he spends his time leaning on the plow while he reads comic books, pausing to take generous swigs from his thermos. The idea that he can read may be the most puzzling development of the entire morning.

The day wears on, and the sun beats down harder and hotter. I'm so thirsty that I imagine waves of pond water spotting the field. I head for them, but they disappear. Rollo stands on the back of the plow, so I have to pull him as well as the farm implement.

Just when I think I cannot go another step without a drink, I hear the sweet voice of Lena.

Fearing it too may be a mirage, a product of my imagination, I turn to face the sound.

"Hey!" Rollo shouts, glancing up from his comic book. "Turn back around, you mule-head! Whaddya think you're doing?"

It *is* Lena. She hikes up her apron and rag of a skirt, then waves at me. She's carrying something in her other hand, but I can't tell what it is.

I whinny at her and ignore Rollo tugging at the reins and shouting at me.

"Rollo Quagmire, you stop right where you are!" Lena hollers.

Rollo mutters something, but he does stop. "Go back to your barn chores!" Rollo shouts.

"It's hot as blue blazes out here!" she yells.

"Tell me about it," Rollo mutters. He takes another long drink from his thermos.

Lena doesn't slow down until she's inches from her cousin's face. "Did you even bother to take Fred in to get a drink of water?"

"Why should I?" he whines. "It already takes too long to plow this field."

"That's because you're slow as molasses at Christmas." Lena plunks down the bucket she's carrying. It's filled with clear, cool water. She jerks the harness reins out of Rollo's chubby hands so my head can reach the bucket.

I drink and drink. Never has water tasted this fine.

"Poor ol' Fred. You'd like to drink the well dry,

wouldn't you?" Lena strokes my neck until the bucket is empty.

I lift my head and nudge her a warm thank-you.

"Aw, isn't that sweet?" Rollo says, in a tone that leaves no doubt that he does not think it sweet at all.

"I have to go back now," Lena says, ignoring her cousin. "But I'll be keeping my eye on you." She glares at Rollo. "Don't you worry none about that."

⟡

Lena keeps her promise to look out for me. Every day in the field, she brings me water. Still, the days are tough, turning over the red Oklahoma soil and enduring the tug and pull of Rollo's reins. Often, the only thing that keeps me going is the sound of my mother's song in my head and in my heart.

Nights, however, are a piece of heaven on earth. Long after the sun goes down, I wait until I hear the gentle tiptoe of Lena's ballet dance steps entering the barn. How I love watching her twirl and bend, flutter and flow!

One night when she doesn't appear on schedule,

I am so disappointed that I have to call on my mother's song. Alone in my tiny stall, I imagine music playing, the song in my heart reaching to my hooves.

Before I realize what's happening, my ears twitch and my tail starts swishing in time to the music. I close my eyes and sway. I prance in place and pivot, pawing the air as if conducting the orchestra in my head.

"Why, Fred, you're dancing!" Lena is standing on the bottom rung of my stall gate and smiling in at me. "If that's not the cat's meow! Don't you dare stop on my account." She claps her hands. "Please, Fred? I could almost hear the music when you were dancing."

I toss my head and shuffle my hooves a bit. But I'm too embarrassed to do more. She's so graceful when she dances.

"More! Encore!" Lena cheers. She hops into my stall and twirls on her toes. "C'mon, Fred. Let's shake a leg!"

I give in when she whistles a tune that makes me want to twist and turn like she does. I show her a few of my own dance moves, rearing and pivoting, twirling like Lena, if not quite so grace-ful as she.

After a while we stop dancing, both of us laughing too hard to keep going.

Lena looks both ways, then pulls something out of her pocket. It's a big, shiny red apple. "Here you go, Fred. I brought you something."

I chomp half of the apple in one bite. Juice drips down the corners of my mouth. It's the sweetest, most delicious thing I have ever eaten.

Before Lena goes back to the house, she whis-pers in my ear, "Fred, I have an idea. And a plan. And a surprise for you. Tomorrow when I come out to the field, you just go along with whatever I do, hear? When I give you the sign"—she waves one hand toward the ground—"I want you to sit down right smack-dab in the field. No matter what Rollo yells at you, you just sit there. Okay?"

I nod, wondering what she could possibly be planning.

She kisses my forehead and says, "Now, you get yourself some shut-eye tonight. And tomorrow, I reckon you're in for the surprise of your life!"

The Big Plan

It's the morning after Lena's promise of a surprise. Rollo is even worse than ever behind the plow. He is hopeless as a driver.

Up and down the furrows I plow, even when Rollo forgets to drop in the seeds for planting.

To amuse myself, I think of my mother's song and sing the melody in my head:

Dance, dance, dance, Federico!
Dance, dance, dance to your own special song.
Sway and spin. Let the music in.

And the world will dance along.
Dream your dreams, Federico!
Dream your dreams, and of course,
Soon you'll shine like the stars above—
Federico the Dancing Horse!

When I reach the end of the row, I turn and face the field. One look, and I let out a horse laugh. The furrow is as jagged as a farmer's saw. I must have been swaying to and fro to the tune in my head. It's a good thing Round Rollo had his head buried in his comic book. I wouldn't mind being around when Rollo's father demands an explanation, though.

About midday, Lena comes running out to the field with a bucket of water. Lena is a true friend. She never forgets about me and always seems to know when I need that drink. It's as if we can read each other's minds.

I nicker a greeting to my friend and stop plowing when she sets the bucket in front of me.

"Hey!" Rollo yells. "What do you think you're—? Oh. It's you again," he says to Lena. "You slow me down."

"Yeah?" Lena says, winking at me. "What's the rush?"

"Huh?" Rollo says.

"Ah, I know," Lena says. "You're in an all-fired hurry so's you can get to the drugstore. I heard about that big shipment of comic books they just got in."

"The what?" Rollo asks, sounding alarmed.

"I hear tell," Lena continues, "that it's the finest box of comics ever shipped this far west. I reckon they'll sell out fast."

"No fair!" Rollo whines.

"Yeah. And here you are with pretty near the whole entire field left. Shame," Lena says.

She turns toward the house. "Well, I'm fixin' to go back and rest a spell since I got all *my* work done. I reckon you'd best be getting back to yours. If you rush, you could finish by sunset. Oh, that's right. The drugstore closes before sunset, doesn't it? Well, I'll be seeing you, Cousin."

Turning her back on her cousin, Lena acts like she's leaving. And that's when she waves her hand down, giving me the signal to sit.

I have no idea of Lena's intentions or why she

desires me to sit down at this point. But I trust my friend. So I sit.

"Say what? Get up, you nag!" Rollo sounds angrier than I've ever heard him. "I mean it! It's your fault this is taking so long. Now get up!"

Lena turns back to us. "What's the problem, Cousin Rollo?" she asks.

"Are you blind? This nag is the problem!"

"I see what you're saying, all righty. Too bad you're the only one can finish a field like this here one," Lena says. "What with all those comic books sitting up at the drugstore and all."

I sit tight.

"That's it!" Rollo throws down the reins. "*You* do it! I'm going after those comics."

"Me?" Lena says, as if the thought never occurred to her.

"Yeah, you!" Rollo shouts. "You got nothing better to do anyhow."

Rollo storms off on foot, no doubt headed for the drugstore, where I imagine he will be quite disappointed in the selection of comic books.

I wait until he's out of range before giving in to the giant horse laugh I've been keeping inside.

Lena laughs too. "That cousin of mine is dumb as a box of rocks, Fred." She pulls an apple from her pocket and holds it out for me.

I stand up before taking the juicy red fruit from her hand.

Lena moves behind the plow. "Okay, Fred. Let's do it!"

Plowing with Lena driving is a breeze. She never rams into the back of my fetlocks. She never jerks the reins. And I know exactly what she wants me to do. I'm allowed to go my own pace, which turns out to be a good deal faster than Rollo's speed.

Straightaway, Lena begins to hum. I pick up my hooves to the beat of her music. The songs are lovely, classical. Often I crane my neck around to see her doing pirouettes, or taking tiny, graceful steps on the tips of her toes, or kicking higher than her head. Her arms move like a flowing stream. Her fingers are as fine as eyelashes. Lena's movements look like her music sounds.

I dance too, though I do try to keep the rows straight. Lena tells me I'm stronger than new rope, which I take to be a compliment.

As the afternoon wears on, I gain more energy, instead of losing it.

Lena talks about herself and where she came from. "My ma was a prima ballerina. She danced at the Royal Academy and all over the world. When she got married, people thought she'd stop dancing. But my pa helped her career. She became even more famous.

"I never knew either of them. Pa was killed in a farm accident two months before I was born. My mama died bringing me into the world.

"Uncle Herbert didn't bother coming to the funeral, although he made it to the reading of the will, all right. He left me in an orphanage until I was six years old. I guess he didn't think I'd be much help with the chores until then. I've been here ever since. I suppose I'll be here until the day I die."

I want so much to be able to talk to her, to tell her she must not end her days at Quagmire Farms. She will be a prima ballerina like her mother. She is still Crystalina the Ballerina.

Lena grows quiet for a while, undoubtedly lost in her thoughts. Finally, she rallies. "Enough of that! Only happy thoughts now, Fred," she says. She returns to humming and whistling.

The sun is meeting the horizon when we finish the last row of the field.

"Okay, Fred! We did it!" Lena shouts. "Are you ready for the surprise?"

I nod my head.

"Then it's time to spiffy up. We're going to a hoedown!"

Horsing Around at a Hoedown

I can't say I have the slightest notion of what a hoedown is. But Lena is convinced that I shall love it. And I would go anywhere with her.

Lena brushes my dingy coat until it's quite shiny. "A horse needs a lick and a promise before going to a shindig like this," she says. "A gal too." She brushes her own hair and washes up in the barn as best she can.

At last, she turns to me. "Fred, I've got a hankering to cut a rug. How about you?"

I have no idea how we shall accomplish cutting a rug, or whose carpet Lena intends to cut.

But doing anything with my friend will be a joy. I nod my head energetically.

Lena climbs to the top of the stall gate. "Mind if I catch a ride?"

I trot over and let my friend slide onto my back. She's so light that I barely feel her up there.

"Fred, you've got one great back!" Lena declares. "Why, I'll bet I could dance up here."

We take off to the dirt road beyond the field. Lena shows me which turns and shortcuts to take.

We've gone about a country mile or two when I hear something. I stop and prick up my ears, rotating them to capture the sound. *Music!*

"I'll bet you can hear it already, can't you?" Lena says. "Keep on now. Just yonder past that set of trees."

I break into a trot, then a canter. The music is like nothing I've heard before, filled with twangs and tweets. It's pleasant, yet exciting at the same time.

Lena lets out a whoop. "Will you lookee there? There's so many folks in that barn, you could stir 'em with a stick!"

A big white barn comes into view. A mix of rusted automobiles and worn buggies are parked on both sides. About a dozen horses are tied out back. And not a one of them seems to care about the magnificent sounds all around them.

I whinny a cheery greeting to the horses. Only two bother to look up. No one offers an answering neigh. I dearly hope that Lena won't make me wait for her with the rest of the equine species.

Lena and I walk up to the barn and peer in through the window. I can see cowgirls and their cowboys, farmers and their wives, stomping their feet to the music. Couples whirl around the barn, the dusty floor transformed into a dance hall.

"So how do you like your first hoedown?" Lena asks. "Truth is, it's my first too. Mind you, I've snuck down here before to watch the action and listen to the music. But this will be my first time to dance."

I kneel on my forelegs to make it easier for her to dismount. It would be such a treat if I could remain by the window so I can watch Lena dance with the other humans. Once she's firmly on the ground, I peer in through the window again, hoping she understands and doesn't take me back to the other horses.

"What do you think you're doing there, Fred?" she asks, her hands on her hips.

I nod. I'm sure she's right. I do belong with the horses, after all. I turn to head back with my own kind.

"Well, now where do you think you're headed?" she demands.

Humans can be quite confusing. I crane my head around to see her.

Lena crooks her finger at me. "How are you going to be my dance partner from way over yonder?"

I perk up. Lena wants to dance with *me*?

"You didn't really think I was going to dance without you?" she asks. "We can cut a rug here just as good as any spot inside, don't you reckon?" She holds out her arms.

I rear up on my hind legs and sway to the music. We've danced together a dozen times in our old barn.

They play a tune called "The Hokey Pokey," and Lena and I do what the song says. We put our right legs in, then our right legs out. We stick our legs in again and shake them all about. We do the Hokey Pokey and we turn ourselves about. I believe I love this odd dance.

Lena sways and twirls to the next song, and I

follow her lead. Soon we're sashaying and do-si-do-ing all around the outskirts of that barn. We square dance, just the two of us. It goes on for a couple of hours, the most fun I've ever had.

And then I have an idea. As much as I love dancing with my friend, I know in my heart of hearts that a wonderful dancer like Lena should be seen and enjoyed by other humans. If Lena could understand how amazing she is, maybe she could regain her confidence—and more importantly, her dream of becoming a dancer.

When the music starts up again, *I* take the lead. Faster and faster we spin. As usual, soon as Lena gets caught up in the music, she closes her eyes. This time, I'm ready. I gently nudge her through the open barn door.

Staying outside, I peek in and watch my Lena swirl and sway to the music. I'm sure she hasn't realized where she is. She's spinning too fast, twirling with the grace of a fawn.

Two by two, the other dancers drop back, their mouths gaping open at this young prima ballerina. Soon, no one is left dancing except Lena.

The music stops. Lena laughs and open her eyes to the thunderous applause breaking out all around her. "What? I—" she sputters, eyes wide at the cheering crowd.

Then with a hearty laugh, she bows. "Much obliged."

Lena races out of the barn and straight into me. "Fred! Why, if you didn't fall out of the sneaky tree and hit every branch on the way down!" I think it's an insult, but Lena is laughing, glowing. "Well, don't just stand there like a bump on a log. Bad as I hate to, you and me done got to get along home."

Lena hugs my neck, then swings up onto my back.

I prance toward home.

I can still hear the hoedown music when I feel Lena pull herself up to a standing position on my back. She is light as a twirling feather in the wind. I tread carefully, and she stays on my back, where I feel her turning and spinning, twisting and dancing under a full moon and a sky full of stars.

The Moneymaking Scheme

A few weeks have passed since my first hoedown. The past nights dancing with Lena have been the best times of my life. We have found music everywhere. Some nights we gallop to the town diner and dance out back in the alley until, as Lena says, "they roll up the sidewalks."

We've found barn dances and hoedowns in neighboring counties. We even ventured, without invitation, to a garden wedding, where a band played.

And when there was no music to be found, Lena and I made our own music in the old barn. I love it best when she climbs aboard my broad back and does her pirouettes and ballet moves as she hums her beautiful music.

On Sundays we attend four church services. We stand outside and listen to the music, swaying and doing our own dance to the lovely hymns inside. As soon as one service ends, we gallop off to the next.

It's the last church we love best. The humans sing and shout the music from their hearts and souls. They even dance in the aisles of that church. The first time we were there, Lena and I walked right in, and not a soul objected. We danced along with them.

At the end of the service, the preacher himself shook our hand and hoof and invited us back. The following Sunday, Lena and I were asked to perform a special number. "Looks to me like you two have done this dancing thing a time or two," said the preacher. "Won't you share your gifts with us?"

"You're dern tootin'," Lena answered.

I felt then that she was indeed gaining the confidence she needs to become Crystalina the Ballerina.

The following Sunday, Lena gave my dingy coat "a lick and a promise," and we did perform at that church. We danced to a tune called "Amazing Grace." I was so nervous I stepped on poor Lena's foot. That made me feel so bad, I stopped dancing altogether.

But Lena just laughed and said, "Fred, who's plucking this chicken, you or me? I reckon I aim to do the leading from now on, if that's all right by you."

That comment brought down the house. The crowd loved Lena.

Now every Sunday they ask for a special number.

I confess that days at Quagmire Farms are as hard to take as ever, with Round Rollo "leading" behind the plow. But Lena packs so much happiness into every night that I hardly mind the days.

☙

One morning as Rollo struggles with the harness, Herbert Quagmire himself appears in the field. I have never seen his face this close up and in direct sunlight. It is a leathery face, not unlike the face of a rooster, with a nose that could slice cucumbers and tiny eyes that look as if they were shot into place by a small sidearm.

If I am not mistaken, his lips are attempting a smile. "Rollo, my boy," Herbert Quagmire says, "wait till you see what your daddy done did. We are going to be filthy rich!"

Rollo drops the harness onto my hoof and stands up. "We are?"

"I've got me a surefire moneymaking scheme that can't miss!" Herbert announces. "Just you wait! This morning, you're gonna see for yourself."

"And we'll be rich?" Rollo asks, his face reflecting his father's expression.

"Richer than rich!" affirms his father.

An hour later I hear a *chug chug, rattle rattle* coming our way.

When I turn toward the racket, I see something green crossing the field and coming toward us. Then I realize it's Herbert Quagmire riding a tractor.

He drives up waving like he's in the Easter Parade. Rollo runs to him and pets the green monstrosity as if it's a Thoroughbred or Lipizzan. The two of them ooh and ahh over the machine and, once again, discuss how filthy rich they intend to be.

Lena comes out to the field, looking lovely,

though barefoot and in oversized overalls. "Hey, Fred!" she says, making sure to scratch my ears before seeing what the fuss is all about. "What you got here, Uncle Herbert?"

"A tractor. Ain't you never seen a tractor before, girl?" Herbert Quagmire elbows his son, and they both laugh, a most similar and ugly sound.

"Not in this here field," Lena replies.

"Well, you have now," Rollo says. "And my daddy and I are gonna be rich!"

"That right?" Lena says, obviously unimpressed. "So does this mean Fred here won't have to pull that nasty plow anymore?"

I hadn't yet thought of this possibility, and a glimmer of hope simmers in me.

Herbert Quagmire lets out one insincere guffaw. "Ha! Not on your life, girlie! I already thunk of that. It's part of my moneymaking scheme. My boy Rollo here will drive this here tractor. And you, little lady, can drive the plow behind the nag. Rollo says he taught you how to plow."

"What about my other chores? And the housework and cooking and—?" Lena asks.

"You'll just have to work faster, girl," Herbert answers.

"Yeah," Rollo agrees. "Can I drive it now, Daddy? Can I? Huh? Can I?"

I want to protest. There's nothing I'd enjoy more than to have Lena as a driver instead of Round Rollo. But I am too worried about my friend to contemplate such a thing. Already, they're working her fingers to the bone. And now she has to do the plowing too?

"Well, you better get to it, gal," Herbert Quagmire says. "You and that nag won't be as fast as my brand-new tractor." He checks the newer, shiny plow, which is attached to the rear of the new tractor.

Lena starts to drive me, then stops. "Rollo, did you have your eyes shut when you harnessed poor Fred?"

Rollo doesn't even turn around. He's too busy climbing up on the tractor.

Lena adjusts the straps of the harness until they're perfect. We set out, and the plow is so much easier to pull now.

Meanwhile, Herbert shouts orders to his son, who can't seem to get the contraption started.

When we're out of earshot of the Quagmire

males, Lena starts humming. It's a lovely tune, and my tail swishes in time with the music.

After a while, we're both swaying and sashaying. If it weren't for the fact that Lena will be overworked now, I would be truly happy knowing I am to spend days, as well as nights, with my friend.

All of a sudden, Lena screams. She reins me hard to the left.

I bolt. Just in time, I dodge the green monster as Round Rollo races within inches of us, spraying dirt onto Lena and me and whooping as he passes by.

"Yeehaw!" Rollo hollers, as if he's riding a bronco. He might as well be. The tractor bucks and jumps under him. He swerves across the field, his plow banging behind the tractor, destroying our neatly plowed rows.

Something tells me Herbert Quagmire's money-making scheme is destined to fail.

Tractor Tragedy

Over the next weeks, Lena and I dance in the field as we plow. But we rarely have time to dance at night. Often, Lena is still doing chores at midnight. I worry about her. If I could speak human, I would have a few choice words for Herbert Quagmire.

Then one evening after Lena and I have plowed our section, she returns me to the barn, bids me good-bye, and heads in for her domestic chores.

No sooner has Lena left than Rollo appears. "Out!" he shouts, yanking at my halter. "You've got work to do."

He drags me back to the field and puts the

harness back on. "Tonight you're pulling my plow *and* the tractor."

At first, I think Rollo must be joking. But I should know better. And sure enough, he hitches me to the tractor that's hitched to the plow. Then he climbs onto the seat, puts his feet up, and opens his comic book.

Rollo cracks his whip. I lean into the harness. It slips up to my neck because it's too loose, and I'm already foamy with sweat from plowing all day. The straps around my stomach are too tight, so I can't get enough air into my lungs.

"Get a move on!" Rollo shouts. He smacks my rump with both reins. "It's hot as blazes out here. I don't have all day."

I manage a step, then another. The tractor creeps forward, pulling the plow behind it. I cannot imagine why Rollo is making me pull his tractor. If the thing is broken, couldn't he simply force me to pull his plow to finish the field? Has the boy not thought of this? I have never heard of a horse pulling a tractor.

I take another step. And another. Never have I pulled anything even half the weight of this load. I feel strain and pain in muscles and tendons I didn't realize I had. My legs feel like trees stuck in quicksand.

I can't trust my vision. Waves of nausea pass through me, and my eyes blur. I think I see Lena far away, running toward us. But perhaps it is my imagination.

Suddenly, from somewhere behind me, I hear a crackling, screeching sound. It takes me a moment to realize that the sound is an attempt at singing. The human voice is the worst I've ever heard, more off-key than a billy goat, harsher than the oink of the foulest pig. This *singing* is coming from Round Rollo. Now I understand what Lena meant when she told me once that Rollo "can't carry a tune in a bucket with a lid on."

The sound is truly horrible . . . and yet . . . it is music. I latch on to that thought and listen, not to the sounds coming from the boy's mouth, but to the beat beneath those screeches.

Yes. I hear music. Fast and syncopated, a type of jostling jive.

I shut my eyes and add my own music to that beat. And soon I feel it in my deadened legs. My tail swishes. My hooves lift. Back and forth I sway, until I am dancing. I pretend Lena and I are at the hoedown. I let myself go, jerking right, swinging left. I am light as Lena. I can almost feel her twirling on my back as I spin and spin.

"Help! Help!"

Rollo's cries break through the music in my head. I wonder why he would be shouting for help.

"Oh, Fred, stop!"

I recognize Lena's voice. So I stop.

Lena races up to me. She throws her arms around my neck, and I feel her little body shake. She is crying.

And then I see why. Herbert Quagmire's new green tractor is toppled onto its side. It lies in the dirt, half buried.

Rollo crawls out from underneath the tractor. Covered with dirt, he's cursing in a language I haven't heard since my final day at the Bar B Q Ranch. "You sorry excuse for a plow horse! Now you've really gone and done it!"

Had I? Did *I* turn over the tractor?

"What in tarnation were you thinking, Rollo?" Lena shouts. Hands on hips, she glares at her cousin, who manages to stumble to his feet. "Why on earth did you hitch poor Fred to the tractor?"

"I had to!" Rollo cries. "If I just hitched Fred to my plow, Daddy would take one look at the field and know I didn't use his tractor. I need them tractor tire tracks in the field in front of my plow. I got this all thought through, and all I wanted was—"

Lena's fists raise as if she intends to use them. "So why, for the love of Pete, didn't you just use your blamed tractor?"

Rollo has lost one boot, but he doesn't appear to notice. "Because the tractor is out of gas!"

"So go buy gas, you numskull!" Lena shouts.

Rollo rolls his eyes like Lena is the numskull for suggesting the obvious. "I couldn't buy gas! I'm out of cash."

"Roll those eyes at me one more time, and I'll

roll that head of yours!" Lena snaps. "Besides, I know for a fact your daddy gives you plenty of gas money."

"Yeah? Well, I bought these here comic books with it. So I had the idea of getting Fred to pull the tractor and—"

Lena cuts her cousin off in midsentence. "*You* had an idea? If you ever had an idea, it would die of loneliness!"

"Oh yeah? Well, you're the one's gonna die of loneliness. Once my daddy sees what this crazy horse done did to his new tractor, he'll send ol' Fred to the glue factory!"

I gulp. I have heard of very old horses being sold for dog food and their hooves used to make glue. These were no idle rumors either.

"It isn't Fred's fault that tractor went catty-wampus!" Lena cries. "It's *your* fault! And your daddy's going to be fit to be tied when he sees what you did."

"The way I see it, Fred hitched himself up to the tractor and—"

Lena shakes her head. "That dog won't hunt, Rollo. Even Uncle Herbert's not going to believe Fred hitched himself up to that tractor. And everybody knows you couldn't drive any worse if you was drunk with one eye shut."

Rollo gets his evil grin, showing yellow teeth. "Then I'll just tell Daddy that Fred went crazy for no reason and attacked his brand-new tractor."

"You lie and your feet stink!" Lena shouts.

Rollo smirks again. "Who's my daddy gonna believe? Me or Fred?"

Lena looks like she's been hit in the stomach. I think we both know Rollo's right. His father will believe him, and I'll be turned into glue, way before my time.

"There he comes now." Rollo waves as Herbert Quagmire steps out of his house and starts toward the field. "Daddy!" Rollo shouts, limping to meet his father.

Lena is crying hard now. "Oh, Fred." She hugs me again. Then she springs into action. Still crying, she unbuckles my harness. "Rollo's right. Uncle Herbert will blame you. Not Rollo." She looks at her uncle, then back at me. "I reckon there's only one thing left to do, Fred."

I feel the weight of the harness drop from my aching limbs. I can't stand to see Lena cry. And I have no idea what the "only one thing left to do" could possibly be.

"You have to run away," she whispers.

Run away? Away from Lena?

"Go!" she shouts. "Run! Run fast! Run far! Don't look back!"

I shake my head no. How can I leave the only friend I've ever had?

Tears stream down Lena's sweet face. "I love you, Fred. You're the best friend in the whole entire world. Now, don't just sit there like a frog on a log. Run! Go! Skedaddle!" She shoos me, waves her arms, and keeps shouting for me to run and never come back.

Finally, with one long look at the best friend anyone could ever hope for, I take off at a trot. Then a canter. Then a full-out gallop.

I run away.

How Now, Brown Cows?

I run all night. Hearing Lena's voice in my head, I don't stop running until I cross into the next county, and the next, and the next.

On and on I journey, munching on weeds by the side of the road, stealing sips of pond water here and there. All that keeps me going is my mother's song in my heart:

Dance, dance, dance, Federico!
Dance, dance, dance to your own special song.
Sway and spin. Let the music in.

And the world will dance along.
Dream your dreams, Federico!
Dream your dreams, and of course,
Soon you'll shine like the stars above—
Federico the Dancing Horse!

I try not to think of Lena. It's too painful. Yet when her face flashes before me in all its kindness and gentleness, I pray that she will come to realize and believe that she was born to dance. And I hope she will find the courage to dream her dream and the good fortune to see it come true.

For days I wander aimlessly. I walk for miles with no house, no human in sight. And very little water. My mouth is so dry my tongue sticks to my teeth. The sun looms large overhead, blinding me. It's all I can do to stay on my feet.

I am about to give up, to lie down and go to sleep, when I see a fence. Whenever there's a fence, there has to be something inside worth keeping in. I focus on the fence and head for it as the sun begins to drop in the sky.

Grass! I see grass on the other side of the fence. It must be a pasture of some sort. And there, perhaps a dozen horse-lengths inside the pasture, is a pond. Not a scum-floating pond either. A clear, sparkling-water pond.

The fence extends farther than the eye can see.

A song Lena and I danced to at our favorite church pops into my head: *So high can't get over it, so low can't go under it, so wide can't get around it. Gotta get through that fence.* I'm unsure about the correct lyrics, but I am sure of one thing. I must get inside that pasture.

After another minute attempting to think when my brain is parched, I know I have to jump that fence. I admit I've never been much of a jumper. At one of the stables where I lived when I was a colt, they had lean, beautiful jumpers, who could sail over gates and fences in figure-eight patterns. It appeared to be such fun that I had to try it. And one day I broke loose from my stall and attempted the bar jump. I nearly broke my leg.

But this is not for fun. This is for survival.

I snort a time or two and paw the ground. Then I take a run at the fence and jump. Up, up I go.

My left forefoot catches the top rung and flings me back. I stumble and fall to the ground, rolling down, sliding down, down, and into a ditch.

I lie there until I catch my breath again. I ache all over, but I don't think I've broken anything. I must get up. I must push myself onto my feet and try again.

It takes me three attempts to stand on my own four hooves once more. How am I ever going to make it over that fence? It looks bigger than it did the first time.

For a moment I simply stare at the fence as it seems to grow right before my eyes. My hooves are frozen to the ground, and my legs are shaking.

Then in my mind, I hear a humming. Lena's voice echoes in my head, and one of her favorite melodies from *Swan Lake* resounds throughout my body as I remember. Lena used to twirl and swirl, then run on her tiptoes and jump. How high that little girl could leap into the air!

With Lena's hum pounding in my head, I twirl, then swirl, then take off at a full gallop. Picturing Lena in the air, I jump as if to meet her there.

And I sail over that fence!

As soon as I land in the lush green grass, I take off for the pond. I think I hear a cry from somewhere nearby, but I don't slow down until my muzzle is deep into that clear, refreshing water. I drink and drink and drink until I must come up for air.

"That's the one!" cries a tiny voice. "He jumped right over me. He scared me." The voice breaks off into crying.

I look up and see a small brown cow, a calf. The only white is on his forehead.

Several other cows step up beside the little fella. They're mostly brown as well, except for one brown-and-white version.

One of the larger brown cows speaks. "Aw, will you stop your crying, Moony? I can't hear myself think."

"Yeah. Don't have a cow!" The brown-and-white cow moos with laughter. Some of the other cows laugh too. "My son always milks it for all it's worth." She cracks up at her own joke.

I manage to smile along. I am quite the outsider here. "I apologize for scaring your little boy," I say, making a slight bow. "I haven't found a drink for days, I fear. And your pond was more than I could resist."

"Mama," the little one whines, "he doesn't look like a cow."

"He doesn't seem like a cow horse either," says one of the brown cows.

The pasture grows silent. And then from nowhere appear reinforcements. Dozens of cows poke up their furry heads and regard me with big cow eyes filled with suspicion.

"I assure you I mean you no harm," I say.

They step closer.

I take a step back. While it is true that I am at least twice as big as any one of these cows, it is also true that I am vastly outnumbered.

The cows have me at fifty to one.

9

Home on the Range?

The brown-and-white cow steps up closer. "I'm Bessie, and this here's my boy, Moony. This old cow is Jingles, my friend."

When Jingles nods, the bell around her neck rings, making it evident where she got her name.

"No, sir. I reckon you're more of a plow horse than a cow horse," Bessie says.

"I have been known to pull a few plows in my past," I admit. "Though I do not consider myself a plow horse. Others call me Fred, but I call myself Federico."

"Well, Fred, welcome to the Lazy Roots and Wings Ranch. Let me ask you a question. What did one cow say to the other cow?"

I'm aware that this might be some sort of test or trick, so I take my time thinking of an appropriate answer.

But before I can hazard a guess, Bessie answers her own question. "What did one cow say to the other cow? Moo!"

This time I join the cows with a big horse laugh. Every time Jingles laughs, her bell rings.

"If you don't mind my asking, why do you wear that bell, Jingles?" I ask.

Jingles starts to answer, but Bessie beats her to it. "Because her horns are broken!" she says.

Everyone except Jingles laughs.

The sun has set, and I'm so tired I can barely graze. But the grass is tall and rich, so I do.

"Well, aren't you the lawn-mooer!" Bessie declares.

I grin, my mouth full of long green grass. These are such nice cows that I wouldn't mind spending time with them. The thought occurs to me that perhaps I could make my home among these kindly cows. "Do you think the owners of your ranch would mind if I spent some time with you here?" I inquire, once my mouth is no longer full.

"I don't rightly know," Jingles answers. "I'm afraid they wouldn't have much use for a plow horse. And the head driver is a hard man."

"You think he's hard?" Bessie challenges. "You should have grown up on the ranch I was born to. Now, that was hard."

"I'm sorry," I say. "Were they so mean to you?"

"Not so much that exactly. It's just that I grew up on the Lazy Double-Q, Williamson Bar-B-Bartholomew Ranch. That brand was a killer!"

I'm fairly confident from the laughter that Bessie is only joking about such a long brand.

Moony ventures up to me. "Good thing you're laughing at my ma's jokes, Mr. Fred. 'Cause if you don't, she'll *cream* you."

Bessie explodes in laughter and pride at her son, who's already following in her hoof-steps.

That night I nestle in with the cows, most of whom choose to sleep standing up, as I nearly always did at Quagmire Farms. But I am so tired, and they all seem so friendly, that I let myself lie down.

Moony stays close, and so does his mother.

"There you are, Bessie." A big brown cow joins her. "Where've you been, girl?"

"To the mooo-vies, of course," she answers.

The big cow doesn't laugh, but eyes me up and down. "Where's your bull?"

"Dozin'," she says. "Bull-dozin'. Get it?" When Big Cow doesn't laugh, Bessie whispers to me, "Don't mind her. She's just got herself a case of the mad cow disease."

The big cow shakes her head, but laughs this time.

Bessie introduces me to her friend, Big Sal, and to another cow, called Natasha. "Natasha is a Russian cow. She comes all the way from Mos-cow."

"So, how many jokes has our Bessie made you sit through, Fred?" Sal asks.

Bessie answers for me. "How do you expect poor Fred to know? He doesn't have a cow-culator."

Sal shakes her head and wanders off.

"You all seem like a nice bunch of cows," I tell Bessie.

"Not a bunch," Bessie corrects. "Herd."

"Heard of what?" I ask.

"Herd of cows, of course," she counters.

"Why, of course I've heard of cows," I say.

"No! A cow herd!" Bessie sounds frustrated with me.

"Now, what do I care what a cow heard? I have no secrets from cows."

Bessie erupts in the loudest laughter yet. "You got me, Fred! Good one!"

That night Bessie is still telling jokes as I drift to sleep. "Knock knock."

I rouse myself enough to play along. "Who's there?"

"Cows go," Bessie says.

"Cows go who?" I supply.

"No, silly. Cows go moo! You really aren't a cow, are you?"

The last joke I remember hearing is, "Why did the cow jump over the moon? To get to the Milky Way!"

In the morning I wake up to the low murmur of the cattle. They're all moving about, shuffling and stirring. Something is definitely up.

"What is it?" I ask Bessie.

"Word is just in. The cowpokes plan to move us up to the North Country. Cattle drive starts this morning. And that means that you, Federico, need to get moooo-ving!"

Cattle Drive—Cowpoke Jive

All around us cowboys whoop and holler from the back of their quarter horses. The horses are athletic and quick, not to mention fast. They race to the far ends of the field, herding stragglers toward the center.

I have no idea what to do or where to go.

"Can Fred come with us?" little Moony asks.

I look to Moony's mother, Bessie, and realize that I would very much enjoy accompanying this herd of my new friends. I believe I'm starting to understand the meaning of those famous lyrics: *"Home, home on the range."*

Jingles shakes her head, setting her bell jingling and jangling. "Fred can't come on a cattle drive, not unless he's a cow."

But Bessie's cow eyes have a mischievous twinkle. "Then we'll just have to make Fred an honorary cow."

I follow every direction Bessie gives me.

"You're brown like a cow," she says, sizing me up. "And you've got four legs. But that's about all we've got going for us. Just keep your head down. And whenever those cowpokes start poking around, you'll have to bend your knees and make yourself short. Got it?"

"Got it," I agree.

Bessie turns to the other cows in mooing distance and shouts, "What do you say, you cows? Can we gather around our new friend and make him one of the herd?"

Consenting moos sound across the pasture. Cows close in from all sides, placing me in the center, farthest from the wranglers. I am touched that they wish to do this for me.

And there's something I wish to do for Bessie, something I've thought about during the night. "Bessie, I've been meaning to tell you something."

"This better not be a joke," she warns.

"I'm completely serious," I assure her. The herd moves forward, and we inch along with it. "I believe you could be the world's first comedy cow."

"What?" Bessie stops. Cows bump into her.

I urge her forward again. "You're by far the funniest cow I've ever met, and I've never encountered a horse with a better sense of humor. You should be telling jokes onstage and making people—and animals—laugh. All you need is a translator. I think you'd be grand!"

Bessie grows more serious than I would have thought possible. "I can't believe you said that, Fred. I used to dream about being a comedian."

"You can do it, Bessie!" I tell her. "You were born to tell jokes."

The day wears on, and the cows work to keep up my charade. They crowd together, keeping me in the center whenever a cowboy rides too close. Bessie gives me the cue to squat down when necessary.

We trot mostly. When there are no humans

around, we talk and walk a bit. I hear more cow jokes than we have cows in this cattle drive. And I am most grateful for my new friends.

Toward afternoon, I tell Bessie and the cows closest to me about Lena. I try to describe the beauty and grace of her ballet. I miss my friend.

Several times I fear that I have been discovered by a cowpoke who stays too long near us and looks too hard my way. Bessie sees it too and calls the other cows into action. Then they stamp their hooves and stomp the ground until we're all covered in a cloud of dust and dirt that forces the cowboys to ride elsewhere.

The sun sets, and still they drive us. Finally, we slow to a walk, then a standstill.

"Is something wrong?" I ask, fearing they're coming to get me at last.

"No," Jingles answers. "Now we get to rest up for our journey tomorrow."

We find a good spot under a tree that looks unfamiliar to me. Its leaves are broader than trees I know, greener too. Grass here is soft and long, with thick blades that taste like spring. For a good hour, we graze in silence, the only sound the tinkling of Jingles's bell and the laughter of the cowboys in the distance.

Smoke puffs up from the cowboys' campsite. Then the low flames of a campfire dance and rise into the cool night air.

Before long, a million stars are shining down on us.

"Fred, did you mean what you said about me doing comedy for a living?" Bessie asks. She says it as if she's been chewing on it our whole journey.

"Every word, Bessie," I say. "You are without a doubt the most amusing creature on four legs— perhaps on two—that I have ever known."

Bessie glances up toward the stars. The glow of the campfire splashes her cheek with light. "I'll do it, Fred. When we reach the North Country, Moony and I will set out on our own. I'll be a real cow comedian."

Suddenly, I hear a twang coming from the cowboy campsite. Then a note. And another. A strumming . . .

"Are you all right, Fred?" Bessie asks. "There's something odd about your eyes. I'd say they have stars in them, but—"

"What is that?" I ask, every hair on my hide electrified and standing at attention.

"That?" Bessie says, glancing toward the campfire. "Why, that's mooo-sic."

I listen, and she's right. One cowboy strums his guitar, and the second cowboy plays his harmonica. The music is soft and dreamy, and before I know it, it's lulled me to sleep. Even asleep, I can hear the notes inside my head.

I wake with a start. The music has changed. I must not have dozed long, but the campsite has come to life. Guitars are blaring, harmonicas zipping, tambourines jangling. Hands are clapping and boots stomping.

And they're playing the "Hokey Pokey."

I bound to my hooves and rear up. Lena and I danced to this song at our very first hoedown. I can almost see Lena dancing to the tune.

I can't stop myself. I hear Bessie, Jingles, and the others mooing for me to stop, to come back. But I can't. I'm galloping toward the flames, toward the music. I turn myself around. I put my left hoof in. I put my left hoof out. I put my left hoof in, and I shake it all about.

Bessie and Jingles follow me to the campsite, mooing.

I know what I'm doing is foolish. And yet, I can't stop myself. I'm on my hind legs, shaking myself about to the beat of the music.

"There he is!" yells a young cowboy. "See? I told you there was a wild horse in the herd."

The music stops.

For a second, I stay in the air, on my hind legs, staring at the cowboys. Then I crash down and look over at Bessie. Her face tells me I've really done it this time.

"After him! If he's wild, he's probably loco!" cries a cowpoke.

"Of course he's loco!" shouts an old codger of a cowboy. "Why else would he come this close to the campfire?"

"Well, don't just stand there!" shouts the one I think is the trail boss. "Get him!"

"Run!" Bessie hollers.

Finally, I snap to my senses. *Run!* I lower my head and take off at a gallop.

The cowboys jump on their horses to come after me. Those quarter horses are the fastest in the world for a quarter mile. And they're not exactly slow after that. They'll catch me before I'm out of the herd.

But the herd has other plans.

Jingles and a pack of her friends trot off to the west, forcing one of the cowboys to turn back and bring them in.

Moony and some of the calves frolic east. Another cowboy turns back.

The entire herd splits into miniherds, and they head in all directions.

"What in blazes is going on?" yells one of the cowhands.

I keep running. Only the trail boss is on my trail. He's closing in. I glance back and see him whipping his lariat, circling it over his head.

Then just as it seems he'll catch me for sure, Bessie appears. She strolls leisurely between us.

"Move!" yells the trail boss. "Get out of the way, you crazy cow!" He yanks his horse to a grinding halt so he won't ram into her.

I look back. Bessie winks at me and begins to graze.

I know I have to go. But before I do, I shout

back to her, "I'll see you onstage one of these days, Bessie!"

Then I take off at a gallop, wondering how many other friends I might have to leave in this life.

Pony Boy

I run away from the range. Again, I race through the night. This time I try telling myself some of the cow jokes Bessie told. Only I'm not the comedian Bessie is. I simply cannot make myself laugh.

Along the way, I find ponds and pastures where I can graze. But I don't stop in any one place for long. The houses get farther and farther apart. Then the farms grow farther apart.

On and on I journey, wondering if I will ever find a place to rest. I miss Lena. I miss my cow companions.

I am bone weary and ready for sleep when I

spot an old shed beside a tiny house. It is as if an Oklahoma tornado picked up this house and slammed it down here.

Yet on further inspection, the house looks clean and as well kept as possible.

I find a safe hiding place among the bushes behind the old shed. Instantly, I fall asleep.

When I open my eyes, other eyes, tiny and brown, are staring at me.

The little person, a girl perhaps half the size and age of Lena, clasps her hands together and exclaims, "Pony!"

I'm so startled I bound to my feet.

The little girl hugs my leg. "It's true! I got my wish—a pony! A real, live pony! A pony friend! And all I had to do was lose a tooth and put it under my pillow." She releases my leg and shouts, "Thank you, Tooth Fairy! My granny said I could make any wish I wanted, and I did. And you answered! I love my pony." Again, she clings to my leg.

I'm terrified that I might step on this tiny girl.

"Oh boy, oh boy, oh boy!"

"Mary? Mary, where in tarnation are you, gal?"

"That's my granny," the little girl, Mary, whispers.

"Mary, you better get in here right now and eat your breakfast! You hear me, gal?"

Mary crouches in the bushes with me. "Granny said I couldn't have a pony until I'm a big girl. I've asked her for one my whole life. Good thing the tooth fairy didn't ask her."

"You've got two seconds to get in here, young'un, if you know what's good for you!"

"I better go, Pony," Mary whispers. "Granny's no fun when she gets mad. You stay here and hide."

I nod. It is my greatest wish to stay hidden.

The house is so close to my bushes that I can hear the breakfast conversation through the kitchen window.

"What were you up to so early this morning?" Granny asks.

"Nothing," Mary answers.

A new voice asks, "Granny?" I'd guess the speaker is a young man. "Did one of the pigs get loose?"

"I reckon it better not have done!" Granny answers. "Now sit down and eat your eggs."

"Why did you think a pig got out, Jeremy?" Mary asks.

76

"I thought I saw one in the bushes when I looked out the window upstairs. Something mighty big."

The very idea! That rude boy is speaking of me! How dare he?

"You probably dreamed it," Mary says. "I'll go look, though. I'm done with my breakfast."

A screen door slams. I peek through the bushes, relieved to see Mary. She glances back at the house and then runs over to me.

But before Mary makes it, the screen slams again. A skinny young man in denim overalls steps outside. He bounces a rubber ball a couple of times. "Mary? There you are. Be careful. That pig could be dangerous."

Why I never—!

"There's nothing in the bushes," Mary says, strolling back to her brother.

"I know I saw a pig over there," he insists. He tosses the ball into the bushes. It rolls directly in front of me. "I'll get it." The boy starts toward my hiding place.

I can't let him find me. There's nothing left to do. I lean down and nudge the ball.

"What the—?" The ball rolls to his feet. "Did you see that, Mary?"

"See what?" she asks.

"That ball. It rolled right back at me."

"You're crazy, Jeremy. It did not."

"Did too!" he declares. "Watch this!" He rolls the ball at me again.

I have no other recourse. I kick the ball this time. It takes to the air in a wide arc.

The boy reaches up and catches it. "Don't try to tell me I imagined that," he says. "Something's in that bush."

"Rattlesnakes, more than likely," Mary suggests.

That stops him. "Rattlers? You think so?"

"I know so," Mary says.

"Well, I'm going to go count Granny's pigs. I'll get to the bottom of this here. You see if I don't."

12

A Horse Named Priscilla

As soon as her brother is gone, Mary runs over to me. "We've got to move you, Pony. Follow me!" She clears a path to the shed.

I follow her. What else am I to do? The door to the shed is rather narrow. I barely fit.

"You'll be safe in here. I brought you some of my breakfast." She unfolds the little apron that covers her checkered dress. Broken, cooked eggs fall out.

I may be sick.

"I'll bring you some water soon as I can. That brother of mine is nosy. We'll have to be careful because he's a tattletale." She hugs my leg again. "Oh, Pony, I still can't believe you're mine, all mine. I've been dreaming about having a pony for so long! We'll be best friends forever!"

Best friends forever. She's a sweet little girl. I can imagine being her best friend. I could watch her grow up. I could protect her. Perhaps I could teach her to dance.

But alas, I know I am not the pony she's been dreaming of. I fear she is in for a big disappointment.

Mary kisses my nose and skips out of the shed. The kiss stays behind with me.

After some time passes, my logic comes back to me. As cute as young Mary is, she is not the boss of this farm. Her grandmother doesn't want her to have a horse friend until she is older. If I had a brain left in my horse head, I would flee before Mary gets back.

But how can I run away from the sweet child? I cannot. So I wait for her return.

It grows hotter and hotter as the morning drags on.

True to her word, Mary manages to sneak

water in for me. Unfortunately, she brings it in a glass made for humans. There is barely enough to wet my tongue.

Mary brings out her dolls and puts them on my back when I'm lying down. She ties a pink bow around my neck—too tight. "Maybe I can find a dress to fit you," she offers.

In the afternoon, she brings me a sandwich. As hungry as I am, I can't imagine how humans eat this. And yet I do find one piece of leafy lettuce to nibble on.

The shed stinks. It reminds me of the tractor smell from that monstrosity at Quagmire Farms. During the long afternoon, I picture Lena, the way she twisted and turned, dancing on her toes. I remember the feel of her feet as she stood on my back and twirled in the moonlight. I hope she's well. And I pray she's finding a way to dance.

Darkness has fallen outside the shed. Not a trace of light seeps in. The shed door swings open, and there stands Mary, adorable in her little nightgown. In one hand, she holds a worn teddy bear. In the other, she has a cookie for me.

Mary rushes to my side. "I was afraid you

runned away." I'm lying down, and she snuggles in next to me. "All day I've been trying to come up with a name for you, Pony. And I have it. Priscilla Pony! Do you like it?"

I don't, of course, for obvious reasons. But I nod.

Mary lays her head on me and begins telling me stories. I love the soft and musical sound of her voice, though the tales are rather bizarre. One is about three bears and a young human girl. Another is about a wolf, a young girl, and a grandmother.

Mary is in the middle of a new bedtime story when she stops.

I wait. When I peer into her face, I see that she's fallen fast asleep. Her hair smells like soap and cherries. She looks like an angel. I remember thinking the same thing about Lena when I first saw her dancing. If I can't have a home with my Lena, or with the cow herd, maybe I really can find a home here with Mary.

"Mary?" I shake her a little. "Mary, you need to go to bed." Of course she doesn't understand. But one would think she would hear me.

The girl doesn't move. Her eyes don't open.

Suddenly, light streams in through the cracks of the shed. The house's screen door slams. I hear footsteps.

"I'm telling you, her bed hasn't been slept in, Granny!" Jeremy cries.

"Where on earth has that girl gone to? She's getting too big for her britches. Mary? Mary!" Granny shouts.

"She's been acting strange all day," Jeremy whines.

Granny yells even louder, "Mary! Where you gone to, gal?"

"I saw her sneaking into that there shed this afternoon," Jeremy tattles. "Maybe some bad man is holding her hostage in there right now!"

Again, I shake Mary and try to wake her.

"Hold your horses, Mary! We're coming to save you!" Granny hollers.

"Where are you going, Granny?" Jeremy asks.

"To get Old Betsy!"

I have not seen another old woman in the house and wonder what use this Betsy might be.

"Your rifle? Goody! I want a rifle, Granny!" Jeremy cries.

"Mary!" I whinny.

The girl doesn't stir. She is the soundest sleeper in the universe.

Soon the door to the shed flies open, and there stands Granny with Old Betsy . . . aimed right at me. "Mary?" She gasps. "Is that you, gal? Are you all right?"

Mary finally sits up. She rubs her eyes and yawns. "Granny?"

"Step aside, Mary!" Granny shouts. "I'll bag me this critter and give him a whoopin' that will send him into next Thursday!"

"What? What's wrong, Granny?" Mary sounds half asleep.

I feel like a coward for doing it, but I attempt to hide behind the little human.

"It's a monster!" Jeremy shouts.

"Where?" Mary asks.

"Behind you!" he cries.

Mary turns around. She grins. Then she laughs out loud. "That's no monster. That's Priscilla Pony."

"What did you say?" Granny demands, still leveling her rifle at me.

"Granny, put your gun down," Mary says. "This is my pony."

"That ain't no pony, gal!"

"Sure it is. Remember? You told me to put my tooth under my pillow and make a wish? Well, I wished for a pony. And the tooth fairy sent me one!"

"You did tell her that," her brother agrees.

"But, Mary, that ain't no pony."

Mary's lips tremble. "Are . . . are you saying the tooth fairy *didn't* grant my wish?"

"Now, girl," Granny says. "I'm not saying that."

"What are you saying, Granny?" Jeremy asks.

"I'm just saying that this old plow horse ain't the one sent by your tooth fairy. That's all."

"You can't take my pony away!" Mary stomps her little bare foot.

"Aw, gal, I'll get you—I mean, that tooth fairy will get you—a *real* pony. Just your size. Besides, didn't you tell that tooth fairy you wanted a coal black pony? That's what you're always nagging me about."

Mary cocks her head like she's thinking. "That's true. I did wish for a black pony."

"Well, you see that?" Granny says. "This here isn't your wish. We'll go into town first thing and see about getting you the pony you're supposed to get."

Mary runs to her granny and hugs her. "Really, Granny? I'm going to get a real pony? A black pony? All shiny and new?"

I feel like second fiddle. Used and thrown away.

"You got it, sugar!" Granny says in her kind granny voice. "The sweetest little pony in the world."

I should be happy for Mary. But I am not. I believe I'm in more trouble than ever.

I follow Mary out of the shed, taking care to keep her between her grandmother and me.

"Bye, Pony!" she hollers. "I hope you and the tooth fairy find your real owner. Have a nice day, Big Pony!"

I take one look at Granny and Old Betsy. Something tells me I will not have a nice day.

To Market, to Market

Bang! Bang! Bang! Old Betsy has no trouble firing at me as soon as little Mary is out of sight.

I gallop away from the old homestead at top speed while Granny shoots at me. Luckily for me, she's a bad shot.

I don't stop running until I cross the county line. Eventually, I happen onto a dirt road, so I follow it. For miles and miles, I don't see a single farmhouse.

After a few days, my surroundings change. The dirt has turned into paved roads. Farms come along closer and closer together. Soon I'm passing houses. Then more houses, and it becomes harder to find grass to eat. Each house is like an arrow piercing my heart, reminding me that I have no place to call home.

Finally, I know that I am close to an actual city, though I have no idea which city.

I'm so hungry that my nose follows the scent of food. I turn a corner and behold a real, live marketplace. On both sides of the streets, humans have set up stalls. But these stalls are not for horses. The tiny booths hold things that humans want.

On one side, a man stands in front of his cart filled with pots and pans. "Cooking pans for sale!" he shouts. "Shallow and deep! Costly and cheap! Come get your cooking wares here!" His words are singsong, nearly music.

Next to him a woman sways in front of a fancy stall. Her dress is long and yellow, silky and beautiful. I imagine Lena in a dress like this. On the woman's arms bangles and bracelets jangle—like Jingles's bell. Scarves hang from her neck. "Get the finest goods for your girlfriend or your wife right here!" she calls.

One stall sells dolls, and I imagine Mary playing with all of them.

There's an entire stall of leather belts, one for

shoes, another for coats. And so on down the road as far as I can see.

On the other side, I see and smell food. It's mostly human food, but I am so starving, it still looks good to me. Fresh breads and jellies, pies and cookies. Bags of powdery things and boxes of mystery.

Halfway up the street I see a vegetable stall. My nostrils flare at the sight of carrots and turnips. An apple cart is being wheeled down the center of the road, where a man stands with a paintbrush and begs people to buy his pictures.

My legs move down the street and toward the apple cart. I am close enough that I can smell the red, juicy, delicious apples the apple man is shouting about. I remember the apples Lena used to bring me.

Closer and closer I get to the cart until my nose … and my mouth … are a horse's breath from a red juicy—

But no. I am not Fred the Thief. I am Federico the Dancing Horse. I am also Federico the Starving Horse. Still, I refuse to take something that doesn't belong to me.

"Stop him!" someone in one of the vegetable stands hollers. "That horse! That wild horse! He's stealing your apples, Manny!"

I turn to face my accuser. "I most certainly am not doing any such thing!" I protest. Then I remember that all this human will hear is "neigh, neigh."

The apple man cries out and drops the wooden tongue of the cart he's pulling. Apples fly out and roll in the dirt. The front of the cart slips opens, and all the apples spill to the ground, bouncing this way and that. "Help!" he screams.

"I'll stop that wild horse!" shouts another man.

"Come on!" shouts a stocky woman in a white cap. "Let's get him!"

This is serious. People surround me. If they could speak horse, I could make my defense. But of course, they can't understand me. They could smell my breath and see there's not a whiff of apple there, but they do not appear to have this in mind. They're running at me with rakes and brooms.

Horrified, I break into a trot, weaving between these misguided humans. Fortunately, humans are a good deal slower than the slowest horse, and I am able to distance myself from their human pack.

I glance over my rump to make sure it's a clean getaway.

Crash! I slam into one of the stands. Hats fly in the air—straw hats, ladies' bonnets, hats with feathers. A cowboy hat lands on my head, blinding me. And . . .

Crash! I bang into what must be a jewelry stall. Gold and silver trinkets roll to the ground. I have to jump to avoid stepping on them.

People are screaming at me. I find myself to be wearing several necklaces. So I shake my head and lower my neck to let the chains slip off. When . . .

Crash! My head rams a food stall. Long, strong-smelling, cylinder-shaped meats wiggle overhead before attacking me. The nasty smell is enough to make my belly ache.

One glance behind me is enough to warn me that what looks like half the town is chasing me.

I make a sharp turn, skidding right, pulling left. I turn again, spot an alleyway, and duck inside. I barely fit between the brick walls of this dark passageway. Quaking from fright, I inch through the passage and wait. It occurs to me that if I'm discovered, I am, as they say, a sitting duck.

I hold my breath and hear the thunder of foot-steps behind me. Angry voices draw closer. Then the footsteps and the voices grow faint.

Pshew. Grateful for the safety of this alley, and unsure where to go from here, I ease to the other end of the passageway and peek out. Little by lit-tle, the tradespeople return to their booths and stalls and carts. Even the apples are recovered, washed, and set out for sale once again.

More and more customers visit the market as the day passes. They're shopping and buying, and having a lovely time of it. I watch them and wish I could stroll the street, safely of course, with Lena and Mary and Bessie and little Moony.

Directly across from my alley is the painter I saw earlier. His back is to me as he stands before his easel and fills a canvas with reds, blues, greens, and every other color of the rainbow. It's like watch-ing magic to see the plain white canvas transformed into a beautiful painting that looks exactly like this very market.

When the man finishes, he puts his painting up in the tiniest booth, next to a dozen paintings that look a great deal like this one. Then he walks back out to the street.

"You there!" he calls to an old woman in a black hat and a flowered dress. "Would you let me paint you? Or I could sketch your face, if you prefer. You have an amazing face, madame."

She frowns at him. "Go away, young man. What would I want with a picture of this face?"

"I'd do it for you for cost," he offers.

"Ha!" says the woman. "Cost, is it now? Then what would my grandchildren be eating for dinner, I ask you? Go on about your business." She waves him off.

I feel sorry for the man. He has a nice face, long like a horse's face, brown hair longer than most men. He's skinny as an old mare, though. And his jacket looks like it's seen better days . . . on somebody else.

"Hey there, Jonathan!" hollers a young woman from one of the vegetable stands. She's not as pretty as Lena, but she's nice looking for a human girl. Her hair is straight and black, and I like the dress she's wearing, a gingham, I think they call it. It would look fine on Lena.

"How do you do, Molly?" The man, Jonathan, tips his hat.

"By the looks of it, I think I'm doing a might better than you. I don't know what's wrong with folks around here. They should be standing in line to have a sketch of themselves. You're that good, you are."

"I'm glad you think so, Molly," he says. "Sometimes I wonder."

"None of that, Jonathan Bean!" Molly says. "You're a true artist, and don't you be forgetting it. You'll get to New York City one day soon."

Jonathan smiles at her. He mutters in a whisper I can hear, but I doubt his young friend can, "And I'll be hoping you'll go with me, my Molly."

I watch Jonathan the rest of the day. I'm reasonably sure he doesn't sell a single painting. And no one comes to have him sketch a portrait.

By the time the clothing merchants start packing up their wares, I am truly starving. That's when I spy a half-eaten apple lying in the dirt, where someone must have tossed it. Without thought, I step from the alley and head for the apple.

"There he is!" cries a little boy. "There's the wild horse!"

Fast as I can, I back up to the alley and retake my hiding place.

But I'm too late. Jonathan the Painter turns and looks right at me, watching me wriggle back into the alley.

In seconds, several of the men race toward the boy.

"Where's the horse, Matthew?" a man asks.

The little boy waves his finger in my general direction.

The painter turns toward me. He knows I'm here.

"Jonathan!" the biggest man shouts. "Did you see where that wild horse went?"

Jonathan clears his throat. "Horse, you say? A wild horse? Well, we mustn't have a wild horse around here. I certainly would have hollered if I'd seen one of those. Did you check over by the courthouse?"

"Let's go there!" somebody shouts.

"This way!" cries another.

They race off like a pack of angry humans.

And I was so sure that painter saw me hiding here.

Once everyone else is gone, Jonathan the Painter turns and grins at me. "You there!" he calls. "I don't suppose you've seen a wild horse around here, have you?"

A Painter's Dream

I stare at this skinny painter, who sent my enemy
in the wrong direction. Why? Why would a human
do such a thing?

But of course Lena would have.

"The coast is clear," he calls over. "Come on
out."

I pick my way through the alley and venture
into the open. He's correct. No other human is in
sight. It's as if the entire street has closed down.

My stomach rumbles, and a wave of dizziness
sweeps through me. My legs give out, and I stumble, but catch myself.

Jonathan rushes up to me. "Easy, big fella." He pats my neck. "I'll bet you're hungry. Me too."

He walks over to his tiny suitcase, opens it, and brings out two smallish, reddish apples. "Here you go. They're even paid for." He bites into his and holds out his hand with the larger of the two apples.

I can't help my bad manners. That's how starving I am. I take that whole apple in one bite.

He laughs. "You really are hungry, aren't you?"

I nod.

He appears to understand at first nod. I must say he is a most interesting fellow. Now that I see his face close up, I believe him to be quite a young man.

"I'll bet you're thirsty too. Well, if you're not in a hurry, you can come home with me. I've got a well full of rusty-tasting water you're welcome to."

This is by far the best offer I've had in more days than I can count. I nicker my thanks and nod again.

"Right you are, sport! Let's be on our way, then."

Jonathan chooses to walk rather than ride. Yet he is overloaded with his wares from the market. Under one arm, he carries a bundle of his paintings. Under the other arm, he tucks his folding chair. The small suitcase dangles from one hand. The load is too much for a skinny human. He keeps dropping one bag or the other.

When I can no longer stand to watch him struggle, I take matters into my own hooves. I drop behind him and grab the pack of paintings in my teeth.

"Say! What's the—?"

With one swing of my neck, I place the pack on my back. Lena herself said my back was broader than any horse she'd ever seen. The bag stays there as if it's on a shelf. Then I take his suitcase in my teeth, careful to avoid teeth marks. He gives in without a struggle.

"Well, thanks, fella! Say, you're one unusual horse. You know that? Sure wish you could tell me where you come from and where you're headed."

I, too, wish I could talk with this pleasant young man.

"I'm headed to New York City," he announces. "What do you think of that, fella? I'll start as a portrait artist on the streets of New York, where there are so many tourists they'll have to stand in line for me to draw them."

I know, like most humans, he doesn't believe I can understand his words. It's the human way of talking to oneself. Still, it is lovely to be included in this way.

He turns and grins at me. "That's what I'm really good at. Painting portraits. You probably saw all of those look-alike pictures I paint for the tourists. People take home my cheesy paintings to show their friends where they spent a couple of days.

"But faces are my true love. I love to draw faces and paint portraits. Molly says I can capture what's inside people when I sketch their faces. I've drawn hers dozens of times, and still I haven't begun to capture the goodness that's in that gal. One day Molly and I will get married and live in New York, where art galleries and museums will beg us to show and sell my portraits."

We walk the rest of the way in a companionable silence. I'm pleased that this nice fellow has such a grand dream.

"Well, here we are. Home sweet home." Jonathan waves his arm, displaying a rather rundown shanty.

I step closer to his "home." Gray boards on the

roof have been hammered at odd angles to cover gaping holes. There's a nice porch out front, but the steps are crooked, and it would never hold me. I'm amazed it holds my slim friend.

"It's not much, but I don't intend to be here long." A cloud passes overhead, but there's no promise of rain in it. "I guess I've said that for the last five years, since I moved here to make my fortune. Or at least make enough to see my way to New York City." He sighs. "I don't know why Molly puts up with me. She's waited all this time for me to get on my feet. I want to ask her to marry me. But that gal deserves a better life than I can give her, someone better than me."

"Hi there, Jonathan! Who's this you've got with you?"

"Molly!" He runs to her, lifts her by her waist, and spins her around. Her long black hair trails behind her like the tail of a fine horse. She really is quite pretty.

"This is Molly," Jonathan says, turning to me. "Molly, this is . . . well, I guess I don't know your name, do I, fella?" He holds Molly's hand, and they come back to my side. "This is Fella," Jonathan says. "How's that?"

I nicker a greeting.

"I'm pleased to meet you, Fella," Molly says. She has a musical voice and reminds me a bit of Lena. "Any friend of Jonathan is a friend of mine." She reaches up and strokes my head, rearranging my forelock.

"I brought carrots and turnips and a good bit of meat on the bone. I thought I might as well pay you a visit and cook up a pot of stew. You don't eat enough to keep a flea alive." She lifts a sack she's carrying. Then she reaches in and holds out a carrot for me. I take a big chomp out of the carrot, chew with my mouth closed, then take the rest from her dainty hand. I nicker again, hoping she'll take it as thanks.

"You are without a doubt the kindest, most beautiful woman in the world," Jonathan tells her. "You sing like an angel, making you the most talented, gifted person in the world. Why you ever bother with me is a complete mystery."

Molly walks over to him. She has the movements of a dancer. Not as practiced as Lena, but very graceful. She stands on tiptoe and reaches up to cup his face in her hands. "My Jonathan. You say something as wonderful as you've just said, and then ask me how I can bother with you? You are the only person who has ever made me feel like I'm somebody."

He takes her hands in his, and they walk into his home. Soon I smell the aroma of stew. And Molly is even thoughtful enough to save me a few more vegetables.

As I munch on the best meal I've had in weeks, I know I must find a way to show my thanks. If only I could figure out how to help them get to New York City . . .

If Horses Had Wings . . .

"Did you ever see so many stars, Fella?" Molly asks.

Molly and Jonathan have been kind enough to include me in their after-dinner relaxation. The three of us are outside under the stars, lying on a blanket. Well, I'm beside the blanket, of course. I gaze at the sky and decide Molly is correct. I can see the entire Milky Way. I can't help smiling when I think of Bessie's bad joke about the cow jumping over the moon to get the Milky Way, or some such thing.

I miss Bessie and her friends and hope the

cattle drive has gone well. More than that, I do hope Bessie will persevere and make it big in cow comedy.

I feel Jonathan's hand on my neck. "Say! You look lost in thought, big fella. Everything all right?"

Molly sits up and begins finger-combing my mane, untangling the mats I've picked up on my journey. "Of course, he's not all right," she says. "He must be lonely for other horses."

"I hadn't thought of that," Jonathan admits.

"Okay, Fella," Molly says in a cheery voice that sounds lighter than Jingles's bell. "You're not the only horse out here, you know."

I pull myself to a half-sitting, half-lying position used by many colts. I look around, but I don't see any other horses.

"You're looking in the wrong place," Molly says. She points straight up. "Up there. In the skies. See that horse flying across the stars?"

Now, I have been known for my excellent vision, but I don't see the horse she's referring to.

"Look harder, Fella," Molly says.

Jonathan sits up and squints at the stars. "I can't see a horse either, Molly."

"Shame on the both of you." Molly laughs a

little. "You're missing one beautiful winged horse. Let me tell you about Pegasus the Winged Horse."

Jonathan and I settle in as if we're children waiting for a story from our mother. As I think this, I get a lump in my throat. If my own mother did tell me stories before she died, I don't remember them.

But at least I have her song.

"Once upon a time," Molly begins, "a wild and free-spirited white horse named Pegasus galloped so fast that he took off from the ground and flew through the air, all the way to the Northern Sky. He was happy there, peering down on the earth and meeting other creatures, like the Big Bear and the Little Bear, Leo the Lion, and others.

"Then one day a young girl, Athena, caught Pegasus and tamed the wild horse with love and kindness . . . and with a fine golden bridle given to her by her father. Athena and Pegasus explored the starry heavens each night, and all of heaven admired the pair, especially Perseus. The three of them—Athena, Perseus, and Pegasus—had many adventures.

"Perseus was riding one evening when Pegasus heard a cry for help. The horse galloped toward the cry, and soon Perseus could hear it too. He recognized the cry of Andromeda. When the woman came into view, she was in a desperate situation, captured by Cetus the Whale. With skill and speed, Pegasus and Perseus rescued Andromeda from the whale.

"Another time, late on a cloudy night after a hard day's ride, Athena and Pegasus stopped to rest at a great mountain, Mount Helicon. Poor Athena was dying of thirst, and there was no water to be found. Angry and frustrated, concerned for his friend, Pegasus stamped his hoof and pawed the ground. He delivered one giant kick, and something wonderful happened. Water sprang up and flowed from Mount Helicon.

"The spring became known as Hippocrene, and it was said to have been the source of all poetic and artistic inspiration. In the end, Athena made her beloved Pegasus, the Winged Horse, into a constellation."

Molly turns to Jonathan and kisses him. "And that, Jonathan, is where you must get your artistic inspirations."

"I rather think I'm more inspired by you, Molly." He kisses her back.

I gaze at the sky, but I simply do not see Pegasus or any other horse there.

"I still don't see that horse," Jonathan complains, echoing my thought.

Molly points to a cluster of stars in the Northern Sky. "First, you'll only see the front half of the winged horse. Second, the horse is upside down. Now, see that clump of stars, four stars making a square? That's the body."

I do see the square of stars, although Jonathan is still having trouble.

Molly points again. "Three stars to the west form the neck, and that bright one is the head.

Next to the winged horse, if you look very hard, you can see the outline of a small foal."

I jump to my feet and stare up. I see it! I see the winged horse. And I see the foal! It makes me think of my cow buddies, Bessie and her son, Moony. I whinny at the stars as if they could answer me.

"Now there's someone with an artistic imagination," Molly says.

Jonathan tickles her for hinting that he lacks imagination since he can't see Pegasus. "Just for that, Molly, you will have to sing for your supper."

"I already had supper," she replies, "which I made myself, if you'll recall. Besides, there's no music for me to sing to."

"What's the matter, Molly, my girl? No artistic imagination?" Jonathan teases. He glances over at me. "Molly will be a famous singer once we're living in New York City."

Molly gets to her feet and stands before Jonathan and me. Then she opens her mouth and sings a beautiful song, something about stars and lovers. Her voice is as clear as the night air, as powerful as the winged horse.

As always, I can't stand still. My tail swishes. Before she reaches the second verse, my body sways and my hooves prance. Then I lose all control and dance, dance, dance. I close my eyes and imagine I'm dancing with Lena at a hoedown or in our favorite church service. I rear up and feel as if I'm flying, like Pegasus, through the starry sky.

Molly finishes, and the night turns silent.

I open my eyes and find Molly and Jonathan staring at me.

"Fella," Jonathan says, "that may have been the single most amazing thing I've seen in my whole life."

"You're good!" Molly exclaims. "Really good, Fella."

She launches into another song. This one is fast and fun. Jonathan springs to his feet and dances with his sweetheart.

"Now, wouldn't we be a sight at the market!" Molly says, laughing.

Jonathan sounds out of breath. "Talk about drawing a crowd!"

We dance another song. And another. And another, until at last, Jonathan walks Molly home.

When he returns, he chooses to sleep outside under the stars. Only I can't sleep. Jonathan's words echo in my pointed ears: *Talk about drawing a crowd!*

And at last I have an idea.

The Big Mambo

In the morning, Jonathan gathers all his canvases. "I'm off to the market, Fella. Help yourself to the grass out back. And apples from Molly. I filled a couple of buckets for you from the well. I shouldn't be too late."

I reach down, pick up his little suitcase, and toss it to my back to help him carry his load.

"Whoa, there, Fella." He takes the case down. "That's a very nice offer. But after what happened in the market yesterday, I think you should stay as far away as possible, don't you?"

I shake my head no. But he insists, so I stop arguing.

"Have a good day, Fella!" Jonathan calls as he strides off, his long legs covering the ground fast, his packages clattering.

When he's out of sight, I make my move. I have a solid sense of direction, if I do say so myself. I'm fully aware of how to get to the market without following Jonathan.

With equal parts eagerness and anxiety, I start out after him. I do realize I'm running a risk by showing myself in the market again. The vendors were not the most understanding humans I've ever met. But I have to chance it.

I take the back streets once I hit town. When I reach my alley, I duck in. I walk through to the end of the alley and poke my head out the market side.

"Oh no!" Jonathan drops his paintbrush and stares at me. "Fella, I thought you understood you had to stay home." He rubs the back of his neck. "What was I thinking, giving orders to a horse? Did I honestly believe you knew what I was saying?"

I nicker to calm him down.

His breathing improves. "I know. It's not your fault you didn't understand."

From my alleyway, I nicker once again. Sometimes it's to my advantage that humans don't realize I can understand their words.

"Well," Jonathan says, "I know you're not going to want to stay in that alley all day again. Here." He pulls an apple from his bag and tosses it to me.

I catch it.

"Nice catch, Fella. Now, stay there." Obviously not trusting his words, he waves his hand. "Stay. Stay. Stay."

Jonathan wanders off. A few minutes later, he returns wearing a large Mexican dancing hat on his head. I recall seeing—well, knocking over—a hat stand with hats just like this one yesterday. Without a glance my way, he goes to his paint case and pulls out a tool of some sort. Then he pokes holes in the top of his new hat.

I watch as Jonathan marches straight for me and sticks the hat on top of my head so my ears poke through. "There you go, Fella," he says. "No one will recognize you now. Come on out."

I am quite sure this hat looks ridiculous. But I

do as I'm asked and tiptoe out into the sunlight. I am pleasantly surprised when the sun doesn't strike my eyes. I may look silly, but the hat does provide shelter, as well as a disguise.

A woman with a basket on her head stops at Jonathan's booth and stares up at me. I don't recognize her from yesterday. "Jonathan, who's this, then? You go out and get yourself a horse? Why, whatever for?"

"Uh...he's...my new partner," Jonathan explains.

"Is he now?" she replies before moving along.

"Lucky for you, Fella," he says, "almost no one ever stops by my artist's stall to look at my paintings. Not so lucky for me, though."

"That's why I'm here," I say, knowing he can't understand me.

What I'm planning will take a good deal of courage. I wait around until the market is busier with people buying and selling. Then while Jonathan sets up his booth, I wander out into the main aisle.

There's no music here, so I must imagine my own. I think of my mother's song, and soon I can hear it in my head: *Dance, dance, dance, Federico!*

And I do. I sway and twist. I rear to my haunches and do a two-step shuffle.

"Will you look at that?" somebody shouts.

"Wilma, you're not going to believe this!"

"Well, I'll be a monkey's uncle!"

"Hey! Come over here, everybody!"

"Isn't that the funniest thing you've ever seen?"

"I don't think it's funny. He's pretty good. He's really dancing!"

I try to shut out the human voices and listen to the song in my heart.

The voice of a donkey breaks through. "Big deal. So you can dance. How'd you like to pull what I'm pulling, you big lug?"

I shut out animal voices as well. Doing one final twirl, I land on my hooves and open my eyes.

Applause breaks out all over the marketplace. Molly is standing front row center, leading the cheering. "Yay, Fella! Great job!"

The little boy from yesterday comes right up to me. Before I can pull my head away, he peeks under my hat. "Hey, I know this horse! Aren't you the one who—"

But I cut off his words as I kneel on all fours and nod for him to climb aboard.

The boy turns to a man who appears to be his father. "I want to ride! I want to ride the dancing horse!" he cries.

"I don't know, son," the man says. He turns to Jonathan, who is now standing beside Molly. "Is this horse safe to ride?"

"Safe and comfortable," he answers.

"How much for a little ride?" the man asks.

Jonathan starts to answer. "Oh, I don't think—"

"Fifty cents," Molly shouts.

"That's pretty steep," the man says.

"I want to ride the horsey! I want to ride the horsey!" The boy begins to wail.

"All right, all right, Matthew," says his father. He hands Molly fifty cents.

I walk the boy all over the marketplace. He's a terrible rider, kicking his legs and trying to bounce. But even he can't fall off my broad back. I keep it slow and steady until we're back at Jonathan's art stand.

The boy's father is waiting there, but I move closer to Jonathan's canvases. I get as close as I can to the paints and act as if I'm posing for a picture.

"Okay, Fella," Jonathan says, following me

to his stall. "Bow down now so Matthew can get off."

I nod to the canvases, hoping Jonathan will take the hint.

He doesn't. "Let's let the boy hop off now, Fella." His voice shakes, and he glances to the father, sending him a fake smile.

I don't want the boy to hop off yet. I try my best to communicate this to Jonathan. I want him to sketch this boy on a horse.

"I want my boy back," the father says.

"My horse will be kneeling down any minute now," Jonathan says. "Don't worry."

Humans. I take one of Jonathan's paintbrushes into my mouth and stroke the brush up and down on a canvas. Surely, even a human can get this clue.

"Oh, the horse thinks he's a painter!" someone exclaims. "Isn't that the cutest thing!"

Then Molly gets it. "For the price of one of these ready-made paintings, you can have yourself a one-of-a-kind picture of your son's horse ride. Jonathan can sketch it for you in no time. What do you say?"

"What a good idea," says a woman who may be the boy's mother. She's carrying bundles from the market and hands them to the boy's father.

"I want a picture of me and the horsey!" the boy cries.

"So do I," says the woman. "Give them the money, Walter."

The father hands over a good deal of money to Molly, who tucks it into Jonathan's money box.

Quick as a whip, Jonathan sketches the boy and me in my hat. It's quite a lovely picture.

When he hands it to the boy's mother, she exclaims, "Why, it's wonderful! You've captured my boy perfectly. Now we'll always remember this moment. Thank you!"

"I tell you," says the father. "It's a bargain!"

"Hey! I want to ride!" shouts a young girl. I believe I saw her with the applecart man.

"I was here before you!" cries a well-dressed boy.

"I was first. You do draw adults, don't you?"

"Form a line right here!" Molly shouts. "Right this way for a horse ride and a portrait. Line forms here!"

All day long, I give pony rides, followed by

Jonathan's sketches. People give me carrots and apples. Molly takes the money and keeps order in the long line that forms. Our line grows all day long, reaching the front of the marketplace.

We are nearly finished when a large woman waddles up. Being a gentleman, I don't wish to sound rude, but this woman is bigger, and rounder, than two Round Rollos.

"I saw your horse here dance this morning. I've always wanted to ride a dancing horse," she says. "Could I get a ride?"

"Well, I . . ." Jonathan has started packing up.

Molly puts her thin arm around the woman's plump shoulders. "I'm sure Fella would find it in his heart to give one more ride."

With a sigh, I lower myself to the ground. Still, it takes Jonathan, Molly, and two other men to shove the woman aboard. It isn't easy getting back up, but I do manage.

"Marvelous!" she exclaims. "Simply marvelous."

I start out at a slow walk. The woman stays centered, casting her weight in just the right places. She's an excellent rider.

"I used to ride every day when I was a child growing up in Cuba, before we moved to the

States," she says, as we weave through the stalls. "Horses and music are my two loves."

I knew I liked this woman.

She begins to sing. Her words are in Spanish, and the song has a lively beat.

"This is a song from my old country. It's called the mambo." She continues singing. I feel her swaying on my back.

And I can't help myself.

I break into dance.

Good Night and Good-bye

"You're dancing the mambo!" the woman shouts. She herself is swaying and swinging on my broad back.

We pass Molly and Jonathan. They stare, wide eyed, at us. "What are you doing?" Jonathan shouts.

Molly doubles over with laughter, then dances in the aisle behind us until Jonathan joins her. Soon a conga line of vendors follows, dancing to the woman's song.

It is the perfect ending to our perfect day.

That night, Molly comes over with oats and apples and a simply delicious feast.

Jonathan counts the day's earnings as Molly cooks up a great-smelling meal for the two of them.

"This is more than I usually make in a month of Sundays!" he announces. "Molly, my love, when did you come up with the idea of having me sketch people on Fella?"

I'm staring at them through the window. Molly glances out at me and grins. "That wasn't my idea, you ninny. That was Fella's."

"Well, thank you, Fella!" Jonathan shouts. "It was one lucky day when you stumbled into my life."

◦~◦

Every day for the next two weeks I give rides to people in the marketplace, and Jonathan sketches, or even paints, their pictures. Molly charges double for paintings. Some humans come to the market just to ride me and get a painting done. It is truly remarkable.

At night Molly counts the money and places it in the little money box.

I am so comfortable with my life here that I

can't help wondering if this might be the home I've longed for. I still miss my Lena, but I know I'll never see her again. And Molly and Jonathan could not be kinder to me if they tried.

One evening before Molly comes over to make dinner, Jonathan joins me outside. He puts one arm over my neck and leans against me. "Say, Fella. I need your advice."

I nicker.

"Thanks to you, Molly and I have enough money to get married now. I'm thinking about asking for her hand in marriage. I'm pretty nervous about it. I mean, we've talked about our dreams together. But that was just talk. What if she doesn't feel about me like I feel about her? What if Molly says no?"

"Well of course Molly won't say no!" I reply. And of course, he can't understand my words.

"Do you think I should ask her tonight?" he asks.

I nod. Up and down. Up and down.

"All right, then!"

Moments later, Molly walks up looking pretty as a picture. "Hi there, you—!"

"Molly, will you marry me?" Jonathan blurts it out.

So much for a romantic proposal. If my young friend could understand me, I would have suggested flowers and an engagement ring. A candlelit dinner prepared by him, perhaps. Soft music playing while he went down on one knee.

"Yes!" Molly runs to him and jumps into his arms. "Yes! Yes! Yes, I'll marry you!"

Then again, there's no accounting for humans.

Molly breaks into song, and the three of us dance. We dance song after song until we're too tired to take another step. It is a glorious night.

❦

A couple of nights later when Jonathan and Molly finish dinner and are counting the day's income, I peer in at them through the open window. A soft light spills onto the lawn, where I graze on sparse grass. I love eavesdropping on their dinner chats and sharing their joy as they plan their wedding.

"Where do you want to get married?" Molly asks. "I'm not sure our church is big enough to—"

"New York City," Jonathan says, cutting her off.

"What?"

"Molly, I've counted and recounted the money we've saved. We have enough to get us to New

York, to have a big church wedding if you want one. And we'll still have plenty to set ourselves up in our new careers. I'll start painting right away. And you can get a singing job. All they have to do is hear you sing. You'll be hired on the spot."

"Oh, Jonathan, that would be wonderful!" She grows quiet. "Only there's one big problem with that." She glances out the window at . . . me.

I shut my eyes and slump, pretending to be asleep.

"We can't go to New York. Not now," Molly says.

"I know," Jonathan agrees. "You're right. Of course, you're right. Fella has been so good to us. We wouldn't be where we are now if it weren't for Fella. We could never leave that horse."

"I wouldn't trust anyone else to take care of him," Molly adds.

"Me either." He sighs.

I open my eyes and gaze in at them.

Molly reaches across the little table and puts her hand on Jonathan's. "We're happy here, aren't we?"

Jonathan puts his other hand on hers. "We'd be happy anywhere, Molly."

"Absolutely," Molly agrees.

When Molly steps out of the house, I nicker to her.

"Hey! I thought you were asleep, Fella." She comes over and wraps her arms around my neck as far as they'll go. Then she kisses my nose. "Good night, sweet Fella. See you tomorrow."

I watch her walk away, knowing that I won't see her tomorrow.

Through the window I watch as Jonathan packs the money away into his money box and loads his paints and brushes for the morning.

Jonathan and Molly are two of the best humans I've ever known. As long as I'm around, they won't leave. They'll stay and see their dreams of New York City fade and disappear.

Jonathan leans out the window and calls, "Good night, Fella!"

I whinny a good night . . . and a good-bye.

18

All Danced Out and Dreamed Out

I travel night and day to put distance between myself and the marketplace. I believe Molly and Jonathan will try to find me, and I can't allow that. They must move on. I picture them in New York City, painting and singing. I shall never forget them. And I hope they will remember their "Fella."

But as day after endless day passes me by, a sadness settles into my soul. The farther I walk, and the more tired I become, the more I wonder. Why can't *I* find a friend I don't have to leave? Why can't I have a home of my own?

I would have been happy dancing at the plow

with Lena. Later, I might have become part of Bessie's herd if those cowboys hadn't run me off. And Mary? All I wanted to do was help that little girl's dream come true, just like I wanted to help Molly and Jonathan.

That's all I ever want. And where does it get me? In the middle of nowhere. Without a home. Without a friend.

Well, what about *my* dream? What about Federico the Dancing Horse?

Dancing. What's dancing ever done for me, except get me into trouble?

I slow to a trot and try to hear my mother's song in my heart.

Only I can't. There is no music in my heart.

There is no Federico the Dancing Horse.

❦

For days I wander. No dreams. No music. What I need is a job. Fred the Plow Horse needs work. Isn't that all we plow horses were born to do?

I pay little attention to where I'm going. I walk with my head down and stay out of humans' paths. I keep as far away from homes and farms as I can. On and on I travel.

When it begins to rain, I barely notice. Only it rains and rains and rains. All day and all night it comes down. I've never seen anything like it.

Still, I *plow* on.

Instead of music, I hear the plodding *schlush schlush* of my giant hooves striking mud. Instead of my mother's song, a new refrain plays in my head: *I need a job. I need a job. I need a job.*

Even at Quagmire Farms I had a shelter over my head and food to eat.

And Lena.

The rain falls in slanted sheets. I turn my face from the wind and trudge on, blinded by watery eyes. And then . . .

Thump!

I crash right into the back of something that feels bigger, rougher, than I. It has a ratlike, hairless tail and wrinkled, rough hind legs that truly are the shape and size of tree stumps.

"Hey! Whaddya think you're doing back there?" The creature turns its head, and I see gigantic, floppy ears. A nose the size of my tail pokes me in the face. It's an elephant!

I back up and look around to size up the situation. Three elephants. A long truck turned on its side. Perhaps a dozen men watch as the elephants try to right the truck. With little success, I might add. Even from here, I can see that it won't work. The elephants are off center, with three pushing, instead of the four they'd need to turn this truck. Consequently, the truck stays overturned.

"Who is it, Harold?" The elephant in front asks the question. She has a sweet, high-pitched voice.

"It's not an elephant," the one named Harold grumbles. "I can tell you that much."

"Well, bless my soul," says the second elephant. "It's a horse!"

"One of the horses from the show get loose, Fanny?" asks a third elephant. She's on the far side from her friend, out of sight.

"My, no," Fanny the Elephant replies. "He's a rather large fellow. And brown." She turns back toward Harold and me. "Harold, introduce yourself."

"*You* introduce yourself," Harold shoots back.

"I'd be delighted to do just that. I'm Fanny, the oldest elephant with the Greatest Show on Earth." She waves to her partner in front. "This is Tina. We're very pleased to meet you. And you are . . ."

"Fed—" I start to say "Federico." Then I think better of it. "I'm Fred. Fred the Plow Horse."

"Well, mercy me," Fanny says. "What *are* you doing out here in the rain, child? With all that hair, you're likely soaked to the bone."

"Pull!" Tina shouts.

They do, but the truck doesn't budge.

Humans stand around, shouting orders at one another. A few try to unload the truck. But they jump back when the truck groans and seems ready to flip all the way over.

"This is not what I signed up for," complains the elephant I rammed into.

"Harold is an old grumbling fuddy-duddy," Fanny explains. "Don't mind him."

"That's right!" Tina shouts. "When the good Lord was handing out brains, Harold there thought God said 'trains,' and he let them pass by because Harold doesn't like to travel."

I laugh and get a dirty look from Harold. As big as I am, that fellow must be twice as big.

But we plow horses are strong. I step into the empty position to complete the four-cornered team. "Here. Let me help." I know they'll never get out of this mud unless I do.

"Well, bless your sweet heart!" Fanny says. "We can use a helping hand."

"He can't help," Harold says. "He's not an elephant."

"Can't put one past you, can we, Harold?" Tina says.

"Hmmmph!" The sound is blown from Harold's long snout. "I wish Ricardo was still here."

"Ricardo was the fourth elephant. He left our little crew a couple of stops back and joined a zoo," Fanny explains. "It was his lifelong dream, though I can't imagine why."

Dreams again.

"I should have gone with him," Harold complains.

"They didn't want *you*," Tina says. "Who's going to pay good money to go to a zoo and stare at *you*?"

"Now, Tina," Fanny says.

"Hmmmph," Harold breathes again. "I still say we wait for the humans to get us another elephant to help us. Not this scrawny excuse for a horse."

Me? Scrawny?

"Now, Harold," Fanny says in her soft, high

voice. "You know elephants are scarce as hens' teeth in these parts. Here we were, the three of us, without a prayer of getting this truck righted, and Fred appears. Don't go looking a gift horse in the mouth."

I like Fanny, and I don't think she and Tina deserve to stand out in the rain all night. I'll get this job done and be on my way. "Are you ready?" I ask, getting my shoulder into position. I'm used to pulling and pushing big loads. I don't expect this to take long.

"Where in Sam Hill did that horse come from?" A man in a cape marches up to us and stands in the truck's path. "What's he doing with my truck?" he shouts in the loudest human voice I've ever heard. He wears no hat, and he's hairless, except for a strip of black that circles the rear of his head. His drenched mustache droops over a round face. His cape waves like a flag in the wind.

"That's Leo, the circus manager," Tina informs me. "Leo is all right . . . for a human."

"Anybody ever seen this horse before?" Leo bellows.

"Does he always shout this loudly?" I ask. I have

seen humans cover their ears to protect themselves from loud noises. Horses don't have this option.

Tina laughs, a mixture of breath, honking, and gurgling, all shot through her long trunk. "Leo started out as a circus barker."

"A what?"

"A barker at the circus," she explains. "They're the ones standing outside tents, shouting to the crowds to get people to buy tickets. They have to be loud to be heard over the circus noise. Leo's the manager now, but he's never gotten the barker out of his voice."

"I can tell." I try to block out his voice. "Ready? On the count of three, Tina and I will push. Harold and Fanny, pull.

"One. Two. Three!" I call. We push and pull. The truck almost goes over. Then it settles back on its side.

It's slippery and hard to keep our ground. But we try again. "One. Two. Three!" I shout.

This time, the truck looks righted. The humans back up and start to cheer. But I know the truck's not conquered yet. "Careful!" I shout. "Coming down!"

The truck slams down again. Groans rise from the crowd of onlookers. The rain seems to pick up even more. Needles of water blind me.

"One more time, elephants!" I yell. "Give it all you've got. One. Two. Three!"

The truck groans and squeals, then slowly swings up. It bounces on its tires and settles upright.

Cheers break out all around us.

Fanny comes down the ditch to meet me. "Bless your little ol' heart, Fred! It's a miracle. You showing up out of nowhere!"

I climb out of the ditch. Tina does the same.

"I'm glad I could help," I tell Fanny. "Good luck to you."

"Where are you off to, Fred?" Fanny asks.

"I'm off to find a job. A plow and a job," I add.

"Do you really have to go?" Fanny asks.

The mustache man, Leo the circus manager, runs up to us. His tall black boots slip and slide in the mud. "That was fabulous and fantastic!" he roars in his barker's thunder. "The most amazing event, an astounding display of power and daredevil bravery! And all happening during the biggest gully-washer rain this circus has ever known!"

It's easy to imagine this man shouting in front of a circus tent. I turn and start walking away.

"You there! You! Horse!" he shouts.

I stop and face the man.

"How'd you like a job?"

Circus Plow Horse

By morning the next day, the rain has stopped. And I have a job with the circus.

By midday, Fanny has filled me in on her entire life story. She's a sweet elephant. I don't ask her age because I am still a gentleman, although now a gentleman plow horse or work horse. But she must be at least half a century old. Still, she works as hard as, or harder than, the other elephants.

Fanny grew up in the circus and has never had another home. She remembers being a young elephant calf, watching her mother unload poles for the circus tents. "Land o' living," she declares. "I've never wanted to be anywhere else."

Tina and Fanny are excited about the circus opening tonight. But I pay little attention to that. I do my job. It's not plowing, but it's similar. We drag and move long, heavy poles. We pull loads and logs and do all the heavy work behind the scenes of the Greatest Show on Earth.

"Have you always been a plow horse, Fred?" Fanny asks. We're uprooting several small trees to make room for a circus tent. The elephants have the advantage with this task. Fanny wraps her long trunk around the tree trunk, gives a yank, and up comes the tree.

Fanny has asked me three times if I've always been a plow horse. Up to now, I've managed to distract her and change the subject without answering. This time I see no graceful way out.

"No. I haven't *always* been a plow horse. But for most of my life, I've plowed fields. I tried a couple of other things." I remember trotting along with the cattle drive, surrounded by those generous cows. I remember Mary and wonder if, at last, she has her pony. And I think of Molly and Jonathan the first time I got that little boy to take a ride and have his picture sketched. "But the other things didn't work out, Fanny."

"That's a shame," Fanny says.

Fanny and I have been given this area to clear. I don't like her doing most of the work. So I back up into the next tree and push, even though the tree bark digs into my rump. Finally, the trunk cracks, and the tree falls to the ground.

"Haven't you ever wanted to be something besides a plow horse, Fred?" Fanny asks, not letting go of this unpleasant topic. "Not that being a plow horse isn't an honorable job. Of course, it is! Bless my soul, where would we all be without the harvest? No grain. No hay. No straw. And humans would starve too. Plowing is a time-honored occupation."

Fanny pauses and stares into my face. Her eyes are round and small, compared to the rest of her. "It's just . . . well, I guess I thought I saw a flash of something else in you, Fred."

"So did I," I admit. "Once." We're quiet for a moment. Then I say, "Shall we get back to work?"

After we clear our area, we join Tina and Harold at the other end of the circus grounds. Fanny and I pass people who are setting up food stands with signs that read: "Cotton candy," "Cold drinks," "Hamburgers," "Hot dogs," "Fries," and on and on. Fanny takes us past a tent with big signs that promise things like: "Fat lady inside!" "Two-headed dogs!" "Three-headed snakes and a snake charmer!" "Vaudeville acts!"

I'm pretty sure that "vaudeville" includes comedy. I wonder if Bessie will ever find her way to a circus. Perhaps she might become a circus cow comedian and . . .

No. No more dreams.

We find Tina struggling to set up a pole that's three times as tall as she is. Harold is off to the side, nosing through peanut shells.

Fanny and I get on either side of Tina and push, push, push, until the pole is straight.

"Gee, thanks!" Tina says. She sits down right where she is. "I am hot as a bear and too pooped to pop. If I—oh no," she mutters.

"What?" Fanny rushes to her friend's side.

Tina is staring up the circus midway, the central path between tents. "Will you look who's strolling among us peasants? Aren't we the lucky ones."

I follow her gaze and see three white horses strutting our way. These are no ordinary horses.

Sweat drips into my eyes, and I blink it away. These horses are true Lipizzans, white as stars, graceful as deer at dawn.

"They're not my kind of mammal, mind you," Harold says. He has temporarily stopped his peanut hunt. "But those are some mighty fine four-legged creatures."

The horse in the center is the most beautiful. She prances toward us, and the other two follow, a nose behind. Her white coat glitters in the sunlight. Even though she's just out for a stroll, her head and tail are held high, and she lifts her hooves as if stepping over low jumps.

"That's Queenie," Fanny says.

"Queen of the Circus," Tina adds, nearly spitting out the words. "She thinks she owns the circus, and we're all her peasants."

"Now, now," Fanny says. "Let's not speak ill of our fellow circus animals, or anyone else."

I cannot take my eyes off this white horse, even though I know it's bad manners to stare.

When the horses are directly in front of us, Queenie stops. The others scramble to keep from bumping into her.

"Hmmm..." Tina sticks out her trunk and

sniffs a bit. "What's that smell?" She bends her trunk so the holes are plugged against her wrinkly chest. "All of a sudden, it stinks to high heaven around here."

I laugh and get a scowl from the lead Lipizzan.

The mare eyes me up and down. Her upper lip curls, showing clean white teeth. "Tell me this isn't the new horse."

"I think so, Queenie," says one of her followers.

"This?" Queenie says, her chin jutting in my direction, making her lift her head even higher.

"That's what I heard," says the other follower.

And then Queenie lets out a giant, and

unbecoming, horse laugh. "That's a horse?" she asks, when her laughter allows her to speak.

"It's definitely a horse," says the first Lipizzan. "See the hooves and the—"

Queenie won't let her finish. "There is no way this . . . this creature . . . and I are the same species! Are you sure he's not an elephant?"

"Funny, Queenie," Tina snaps. "I'd like to see you carry a load like Fred here does."

"Well, you won't," Queenie snaps back. "Because I am not a work horse. *I* am a performing horse! Come on, girls. Let's allow these . . . *elephants* to get back to work!"

Queens and Princesses

Queenie and her friends prance away. They glance back and then erupt into horse laughs.

"That horse," Tina complains. "She steams my trunk! I don't suppose you've met Princess yet, have you?"

I shake my head. "Another Lipizzan?"

"Human," Tina says. "Barely. She's a human version of Queenie."

"I don't like to speak ill of any soul," Fanny says, "but Tina's right. Those two, Queenie and Princess, Queenie's rider, are cut from the same cloth. Spittin' images."

"Those two may be the headliners of the circus," Tina says. "But they're also the head cases of the circus. They act like they think they're better than everyone else. Gets my goat, I'll tell you!"

"They're sure purty," Harold finally chimes in.

"And don't they know it!" Tina says. "Purty stuck on themselves, that is. Princess and her human gals are just as bad as the horses."

"Not all of them," Fanny says. "That new girl is as sweet as she can be."

"She brings us peanuts," Harold says. "Buys them with her own money too."

"I think she's the best rider in the show," Tina says. "A lot better than Princess. I heard that Princess treats the new girl like dirt. Probably jealous of her already. She's only been here a couple of weeks, so she has to ride Diamond, the third horse you saw. Diamond's bumpy. I don't know how that new girl can stay up on him."

❦

Fanny and I work together the rest of the day, clearing and helping set up the circus tents. That elephant is so smart and personable that I think she could do a lot of other jobs.

"Fanny, if you don't mind my asking, and since you did ask me, haven't you ever thought about doing something else with your life?"

Fanny snorts. "Mercy, no! I would miss the circus life. The thrill of it all when the lights go on."

As if they've been listening to Fanny the Elephant, the lights do go on all across the midway. They twinkle from strings hung crisscross over the main aisle. Torches of fire hang at each tent's entrance.

We stand on a hill and look down on the scene. "What else would you miss, Fanny?"

"So many things, sweetie. The squeals of the children when they first see the big tent. The shouts of the barker, calling folks to come inside and take a peek. The midway smells of corn on the cob, popcorn, hot dogs, and peanuts, of course."

Fanny's eyes look misty. She sighs. "No, Fred. I was born to be a circus elephant. That must be why I'm so happy here. I couldn't stand it if I stopped seeing the joy on those children's faces. Circus joy, that's what it is. And I got it too, in my veins."

As we watch the grounds swell with humans, I try to work things out in my head. What about this feeling of being born to do something? Do some plow horses feel born to plow? It had never occurred to me that for some horses, plowing *was* their dream. Maybe plowing made them feel worthwhile, the way Fanny feels about her work. I do remember one old mare at the first farm I ever worked. Every morning, she headed for the field with a smile on her face. And in the evening, she and a big bay gelding used to talk about their straight rows and how much of the field they'd been able to finish. They seemed happy to me.

It's all so confusing. If I were born to be a plow horse, wouldn't I have been content and happy plowing?

Why wasn't I? Why was I happiest when I was dancing?

The circus grows louder and louder. I can see what Fanny means about the barkers. Their cries can be heard all over the circus: "Come see the five-hundred-pound fat lady!" "Ladies and gentlemen! In this tent is the world's strongest man!" "Tickets! Tickets! Tickets!"

I have to admit it's rather exciting. Children dart from place to place, laughing, while grown-ups stroll the midway arm in arm.

I've almost forgotten about Fanny, when she taps my shoulder with her trunk.

"Are you all right, Fred?" she asks.

I nod. "Just a lot on my mind, I suppose."

A breeze kicks up, and with it comes the sound of music. I hold my breath and find I have to swallow tears.

"You hear the music?" Fanny asks.

I manage a nod.

"It's heavenly, isn't it?" she says.

"Where's it coming from?" There's something familiar about the slow, classical melody floating over the circus grounds. I feel as if I'm being washed by the music. It covers the red dust of an Oklahoma field, the black dirt of the cattle drive, the splintery floor of that old shed, and the rocky ground of the marketplace.

"It's coming from the main tent, dear," Fanny says. "The horses must be about to perform."

"The horses?" I ask.

"And their riders. Queenie and Princess and the others. The dancing horse act. You should go, Fred," Fanny urges. "Wouldn't you like to see the horses dance?"

Would I? Do I want to see other horses doing

what I used to dream about? . . . What I *still* dream about?

"Come on. I'll show you." Fanny nudges me with her trunk, then guides me right up the midway. Tiny flags wave in the breeze as we pass tent after tent.

When we reach the biggest tent, Fanny says, "Well, this is it." She motions toward the entrance, where a tent flap is pinned back.

I try to see inside. It isn't easy. People are streaming in. I see the metal bleachers the elephants and I hauled over, and they're teeming with humans. The tent is filling fast.

Suddenly, Queenie bursts out of the tent and trots past us, nearly running over a family with six redheaded kids, including a baby. "I refuse to perform under these conditions! I am Queenie, the star of the show! I've tried to tell these humans that I want new costumes. But do I get them? No!"

I'm not sure if she's talking to her two friends, who cower just inside the tent. Or to herself.

Leo, the circus manager, trails behind her. "Queenie, I can't have you walking out on me! Not again!" He's shouting louder than the barkers. I have a feeling part of his volume comes from anger.

Queenie spins around to face him, and he takes a step back. She stretches out her neck and lays her ears back flat. She's apparently angry as well. "I'm not carrying that rude girl, Princess, and you can't make me!"

I have to wonder if this horse realizes that humans don't understand her words.

Queenie shows her teeth to Leo and shouts, "I quit!" Then she turns and gallops off.

Leo points at the disappearing white horse and shakes his finger. "You're fired!"

On with the Show!

We all watch Queenie until she's completely out of sight.

"Now what am I going to do?" Leo shouts.

Tina and Harold have joined Fanny and me.

"Was that Queenie?" Tina asks. "Did Leo just fire her?" Tina is laughing.

"Or she quit," Fanny says. "Hard to say which."

Harold is still looking at the spot where Queenie could last be seen. "She sure was purty," he says.

A young girl with red curls piled on top of her head storms out of the tent. She's wearing white tights and a pink ballet tutu. "Leo!" she screams.

"Now what am I supposed to do?" She stomps her foot.

"That's Princess," Fanny explains.

"I guessed as much." If Queenie were to turn into a human, this is the human she would become. They even have the same scowl.

"Right-o!" Leo barks. "Queenie was your ride, wasn't she? Yes. That does present a problem."

"I'll just take Ruby's horse," Princess announces.

A girl dressed just like Princess is standing behind her. "But if you ride my horse, what will I ride?" This must be Ruby.

"That's not my problem," Princess says.

"Princess!" Ruby whines and throws a little tantrum, stomping her feet and wailing.

Princess glances around at the crowd waiting to get into the tent. "Oh, stop bawling, Ruby!" Princess shouts. "You can ride what's-her-name's horse. That new girl. She's been riding Diamond. You take Diamond, and I'll take your horse, Royal. That should put the new girl in her place once and for all."

During this conversation, Leo the circus manager has not been managing. "Wait. Girls! Girls? I'm not sure that's fair to the new girl. She's—"

But Princess and Ruby have gone back inside

the tent, no doubt to give the unfortunate new girl the good news.

"That poor gal's going to be disappointed not getting to ride in center ring tonight," Fanny says. "She's been practicing and practicing."

I move in closer to the tent. I want to hear that music again. And I admit I'm curious as to how the new girl will handle the news.

Tina gives me a hard shove with her trunk. "Go on in, Fred. You can tell us what's going on."

I step inside. It takes a minute for my eyes to adjust to the lights. Right away, in the smaller arena, probably the practice arena, I spot Princess and Ruby and another girl dressed just like them.

The third girl is standing on one of the white horses. Her back is to me, and the other two girls are yelling at her from the ground. I can tell she's as comfortable standing on the back of that horse as she'd be standing on the ground. I remember what Tina said about her being the best rider. I believe it. Simply bending down to talk to the other two girls, this girl is as graceful as an angel.

There's something familiar about her . . .

Suddenly, Princess reaches up, grabs the new girl's ankle, and pulls it out from underneath her.

The poor girl falls and lands on her stomach with a *thump*. Her body bounces in the sawdust of the arena.

I can't believe it! I gallop into the arena to keep Princess from harming the girl further.

The girl appears to be struggling to get her breath. Just as I arrive at her side, she turns over onto her back. When she looks at me, her green eyes grow as round as the full moon.

It's Lena. The new girl is my Lena!

"Fred? Is it really you? It can't be. But it is!" She jumps up and flings her arms around me. "You're here! I'm not dreaming. You're really and truly here!" She draws back. "Unless I hit my head too hard and I'm crazier than a june bug in August."

I nudge Lena and nicker.

"It *is* you, Fred! I'd know that nicker anywhere!"

I nuzzle her and feel warm tears well up in my throat. *Lena. My* Lena. I thought I'd never see her again.

"Well, you can knock me in the teeth and call me Mabel!" Lena exclaims. Tears are streaming down her cheeks. She scratches me behind the ears, just like in the old days. "I've missed you so much, Fred! You have no idea."

She's wrong about that. As hard as I've tried not to think about her, the pain of missing Lena has always been there, in my heart, with my mother's song.

"I've never forgotten you, Fred," Lena continues. "I've missed you something awful. You're the reason I'm here, you know!"

This confuses me, but I listen.

"You were bound and determined I oughta keep dancing. You gave me the guts to dream and the gumption to do something about it. I finally done run away from Uncle Herbert, Cousin Rollo, and that sorry excuse for a farm. And none too soon neither.

"When the circus came to town, I snuck off and joined up. For the last couple of weeks, I've been dancing on the back of one of them white horses. They're pretty snooty. But I do love dancing in the circus."

I'm so proud of Lena for following her dream. And I'm pleased to hear her say I had a small part in that. Somehow, that's better than reaching my own dream. I feel like I did when Bessie announced she was going to be a cow comedian. Or when Mary realized she was getting a pony. Or like I felt when Jonathan and Molly got enough money to go to New York.

Only I feel that joy a hundred times over for my Lena.

Lena presses her soft cheek against my neck, and I could stay like this forever.

"Circus dancing is a hoot, Fred," she says. "Only no horse has ever been as good as you at dancing. Those white horses with their skinny backs can't hold a candle to you. Why, I can't even do a pirouette without falling off."

Leo runs up to us. "Are you all right, Lena?" he shouts. "I saw what Princess did to you. She shouldn't have done that, and I told her so. But those two gals have been here longer than you. So if we've just got two horses, I'm afraid I have to let them ride tonight."

Lena hangs her head, then nods at him.

"I'm awful sorry," Leo continues. "I know I promised you center ring tonight, but without a horse . . . well, I knew you'd understand."

Lena nods again, and sniffs. "Yeah. I reckon," she says.

I can't stand seeing Lena sad. Tonight was going to be her big moment in center ring. And now she can't even ride? Just because that Queen horse stormed off?

It's not fair. No one dances better than Lena. If they could just see her . . .

Lena reaches up and scratches my back. I recall the feel of her toes as she danced there, light as a feather.

And then the thought comes: *Lena could dance there again.*

But no. She couldn't. *I* couldn't. I've stopped dancing. Haven't I? And anyway, how long has it been since Lena and I danced together?

No. No. No. I'd just be setting myself up again, shooting for my dancing dream and missing once more.

I glance back at Lena. She's watching the other two girls ride their white horses into the center ring.

Circus music starts up again, louder now. It's lovely and lively. Something inside of me sparks, lights, then bursts into bright flames. *Music!* I can't keep still. My body moves to the beat.

Lena laughs through her tears. "Aw, Fred. Look at you swaying to that music! You just can't help yourself, can you? You were born to dance."

Born to dance. I think about those words. I chew them. And then I swallow.

I *am* a born dancer! Dancing is my destiny!

I throw myself into the music and dance.

From the tent entrance, my elephant friends cheer.

I whinny to them. Then I get down on my knees until I'm eye to eye with Lena. I lock my gaze onto hers and won't let go.

Lena shakes her head slowly. "Fred, you're not thinking what I think you're thinking, are you?"

I am fairly certain that I am. I nod.

"No siree! Do you want Princess and her gals and them horses to run us clean out of the circus?"

I use my head to motion Lena to climb aboard. I know the music must be filling her the same way it fills me. *She* was born to dance too.

Lena narrows her eyes at me. Slowly, her lips curl into a giant grin. She reaches up to her head-dress, pulls out a handful of feathers, and sticks them into my mane. Then my Lena hops aboard. "As they say in the business, Fred, on with the show!"

I spring to my feet and prance to the center arena, where two white horses are cantering in a tight circle. Princess and Ruby stand on their horses' backs. But I am surprised to see that they are not really dancing.

I fall in behind the horse they call Diamond. He glares at me over his rump, then kicks out his hind leg and catches me on the chest. His hoof is so small I barely feel it.

Lena gasps. "Are you all right, Fred?" she shouts down.

In answer, I do a little twirl to give Diamond time to pull ahead and out of our way. The crowd explodes with hurrahs and bravos.

"What do you think you're doing, new girl?" Princess shouts from behind us. "Get out of this ring right now!"

Her mount, Royal, mutters a few choice words and threats of her own. Then she gallops up behind us and bites my rump. Princess laughs, and the pair move up beside us. Then the girl reaches over and shoves Lena.

The crowd gasps.

Lena manages to keep her balance. Then I feel her spin and twirl on my back and deliver a well-timed ballet kick to Princess's leg.

The kick barely touches Princess, but the girl lets out a yelp and drops back in behind us.

"Wahoo!" Lena cries. "This is more fun than a pond full of penguins!"

With the other horses and riders taken care of, Lena and I fall into our old dance steps. We move as one, dancing around center ring, flying like Pegasus the Winged Horse.

How did this happen? My mind swirls with thoughts of Bessie and Moony, of little Mary, of Jonathan and Molly, and of Lena. It was helping them fulfill their dreams that made me end up here—right here, fulfilling my own dream.

In the limelight now, Lena and I swirl and twirl to the wild applause of the circus crowd. It feels as if my friend and I have been dancing like this forever.

I have found my home at last.

We're almost to the end of our performance when the circus music grows dim, and my own music kicks in loud and true. Then in my heart, I hear my mother's song:

Dance, dance, dance, Federico!
Dance, dance, dance to your own special song.

Sway and spin. Let the music in.
And the world will dance along.
Dream your dreams, Federico!
Dream your dreams, and of course,
Soon you'll shine like the stars above—
Federico the Dancing Horse!

From that night on, the Greatest Show on Earth has a new headliner. If you come to the circus, you can't miss the giant banner over the main tent. It reads:

CRYSTALINA THE BALLERINA
AND
FRED THE DANCING PLOW HORSE

And don't miss these other wild and woolly

Angus MacMouse Brings Down the House

When a music-loving mouse runs onstage at the opera, he scares the soprano so much that she sings her highest note yet! Soon Angus MacMouse helps her become a worldwide star—and he has big dreams for himself too.

The Pup Who Cried Wolf

Lobo is a tiny Chihuahua with a big dream—to join a wolf pack. When the family goes to Yellowstone National Park, Lobo finally has the opportunity to find his wolf brothers. But is the wild really where a feisty little five-pound pup belongs?

Monkey See, Monkey Zoo

When a little boy leaves his backpack behind at the zoo, Willa the monkey gets her chance to see what life is like outside her cage. After an exciting escape, she sets off on a journey to return the backpack—with plenty of monkey business along the way!